TALES AS TALL AS A SUNFLOWER

BY STEPHEN BUTTERMAN

Bellissima Publishing, LLC
Jamul, California
www.bellissimapublishing.com

Copyright © 2009 by Bellissima Publishing, LLC

All rights reserved. No part of this book may be reproduced or transmitted in any form or by any means, electronic or mechanical, including any photocopying, or recording, or by any information or storage retrieval system, without permission from the publisher and author.

IBSN 1-935118-74-9
First Edition

To My Nephews & Nieces

Introduction

Do you love to garden, and do you also enjoy a tall tale once in awhile? If the answers to these questions are yes, then you will really enjoy this book. Filled with gardening truths, each tale is filled with introspection about the world and life in general. And warm with family and friends in a realistic setting, each story of reminiscence flows into the next.

This is Stephen Butterman's first book with Bellissima, and we certainly hope it will not be his last. Sit in the garden on a summer day and read this book, or read it in winter as you dream of a spring garden. The stories take place in the Midwest, with a hint of the California coast that will make you smile. This is a perfect book for subway, train or plane reading, and a real touch of Americana, and you do not have to live in the Midwest or in California to really love these stories!

The politics in the mix are funny and fun, and if you want to know how vegetable gardens relate to either flowers or politics, you will just have to read this book! Ask yourself as our author did if a ladybug is always a lady, and why peppers are so saucy and hot.

If you talk to your plants, or make deals with gray squirrels, this is a must read for you; and even if you do neither of these things, you will not want to miss out on this funny, funny book of short stories that will surely make you laugh and smile.

Tales As Tall As A Sunflower

By Stephen Butterman

Tales Taller than Sunflowers

CHAPTER ONE

Saving the Snails

I've enjoyed many pleasurable experiences in my Midwestern vegetable garden. I mean, I've trenched it out during flood years and spent hours hauling water to it during draught years; and I don't know for what more a gardener could ask, unless it is utilizing unique combinations of hope, prayer, praying mantises, lady bugs, hard labor and a variety of voodoo hexes against weed forests and bean-eating bugs during the rare *good* year.

So naturally I looked forward to helping my charming cousin Vicky plan, plant and patrol a Southern California garden. I visualized the potential pleasures of protecting it against raging brush fires, massive mudslides and teeth-rattling earthquakes. Yes, growing a Californian garden would likely prove relatively relaxing.

2

Tales Taller than Sunflowers

First, let me tell you about sweet cousin Vicky. That girl is a hardcore environmentalist with a capital M-E-N-T-A-L. She would not only save the whales, but would furthermore elect them to the Senate! She owns and studies books about liberating innocent animals from evil experimental labs. She owns and studies books about liberating defenseless trees from tree-molesting logger-monsters—by driving steel spikes into them (the trees, I hope). I can imagine her now, in her most loving maternal tone: "This is going to hurt me more than it hurts you [*pound pound*]; but it's for your own good [*pound pound*]." (Whether the defenseless trees would rather become fake vinyl siding than have steel spikes lovingly pounded into them, is apparently not an issue.)

Being the busy loafer that she is, Vicky could never find the time to execute such exciting strategies. She does, however, recycle my aluminum cans, thus sending several third-world aluminum-exporting countries into mild recessions. She meanly scowls at air-despoiling cigarette smokers (like her mother and me) and she also saves leafy beings from waste and annihilation.

That's right. Vicky may *not* be an actual liberator of animals or trees, but she *is* a First Class Leafy Being Liberator. It seems that people in L.A.'s ritzy neighborhoods routinely pull up (or more likely have their gardeners pull up) perfectly healthy plants so they can plant different varieties in their places. On certain smoggy mornings the pulled-up (but otherwise fine and potentially happy leafy beings) sit on curbsides throughout the ritzy neighborhoods, patiently waiting not for a stretch-limo to Dodger Stadium or Sac's Fifth Avenue, but for a common garbage truck to a local dump.

Enter Vicky, the spirited if not fanatical Leafy-Being Libber. No, she *does not* toss tomato juice or maple syrup on the unfeeling, unenlightened ritzy people. However, she *does* stalk certain ritzy neighborhoods certain smoggy mornings and bravely liberates not-fatally-pulled plants from the trash piles, presumably hugs and kisses them, and rushes them off to affectionately prepared soil at her boyfriend's and mother's yards, as well as to many of her neighbors' yards. There she transplants them and nurses them back to health and blossom.

Not only are the leafy beings saved thusly, but her boyfriend's and mother's neighborhoods look more lush and lovely as a result. Indeed, the well-tended flora *throughout* Los Angeles amazed me. Riding one day through Hollywood (where Vicky works as a minor film-editor and major office illuminator) I commented on this lushness.

"Do many people garden back in Ohio?" she asked.

Now when I think of gardening Ohio-style, I don't think of the hedges, roses, lilies, begonias and petunias that surrounded us in

Tales Taller than Sunflowers

Hollywood. I think of beans, peppers, potatoes, tomatoes and cucumbers—you know, lovely *and* practical leafy beings.

So I responded thusly: "Sure, *lots* of people do, but we don't do as much decorative gardening as vegetable gardening."

"*Decorative* gardening?" She asked as she paused for a long moment, eyes flashing. "Well, I guess you *could* [if you're a hayseed from Ohio] call it 'decorative' gardening."

(Although it must have been 80 degrees out, it felt like frost formed on the dashboard.)

Sure enough, not to be insulted by a hayseed cousin from Ohio who possibly, probably and almost *certainly* knew little about growing things other than watching the grass grow weekend nights, the very next evening she announced she and I would plant a *vegetable*—actually, she said "non-decorative"—garden. I could hardly sleep through my exciting waking-dreams of garden threatening brush fires, mudslides earthquakes.

Vicky's mother's yard was huge for a Southern California yard, about as big as my carrot patch in Ohio. Nonetheless, the next morning we selected a likely corner of that yard and made plans to ss plant squash, bean, corn, carrot, lettuce, tomatoes and pepper and cucumber plants, one of each.

In an effort to make up for my insensitive tongue-slip of the previous day, I offered to turf, spade and hoe the soil. Dear Vicky wouldn't hear of such unnecessary manual labor. She said she'd rent a rototiller instead.

"But I can remember our Grandfather remembering his Grandfather remembering *his* Grandfather working an entire farm by hand," I protested.

But that *didn't* matter. We rototilled that postage-stamp sized plot—estimated market value: $250,000, or so. We gently planted and joyfully watered. We continued to water, and young plants emerged and did what healthy young plants do; and that is to grow.

No drought, no flood, no brush fire, mudslide or earthquake threatened them and neither did any weed-forests or bean-devouring bugs. What threatened them were veggie-plant devouring snails! Mornings we would examine the young garden and find squash, bean and lettuce leaves chomped down to stumps. As the sneaky snails feasted—like vampires—only at night, we would not have easily identified the culinary culprits had we not found several of them in the moist shade nursing apparent hangovers, green spittle at the corners of their greedy little mouths.

We *had* to do something.

"Use slug-&-snail poison," suggested Vicky's mother, my Aunt Lil, an earthy, practical Midwest native. "I've noticed it at the store."

"No way!" retorted 100% Natural Vicky, eyes flashing.

"Or surely there's a natural predator that we could buy and let loose in the garden?"

"Are you *joking*?" asked save the-whole-world-including-sharks-and-tigers-should-be-vegetarian Vicky, her eyes even more brilliantly flashing.

Vicky's boyfriend Jason, who likely considered our garden a green pain to begin with, pitched in this idea: "I've heard that if you put a bowl of beer in the ground, slugs and snails will crawl into it and drown."

"What a silly, not to mention *brutish* suggestion," I literally hissed, my eyes flashing if not glowering.

(You see, the only beer on the premises belonged to me, and I had none to spare for freeloading snails.)

Then I recalled a tidbit of information that *might* save our plants, the snails and (most importantly) my beer.

"I remember reading that there's a certain type of mulch that snails won't cross," I said. "Surrounding your plants with it is like a surrounding a fort with a crocodile-infested moat!"

Vicky hit the Internet and quickly found out what type of mulch it was, cypress. . . cedar. . . I forget. (We hayseed Ohioan gardeners usually use non-decorative leaves or straw as mulch.) Anyway, we obtained (meaning Aunt Lil bought) the moat-like mulch, placed generous amounts around each plant, patted one another on the back (Vicky a tad vigorously, I thought) enjoyed deep, untroubled dreams, and awakened to an *astounding* failure. Perhaps the snails nimbly leaped over the mulch. Perhaps they tunneled under it. Perhaps the mulch strategy lacked credence regarding these tenacious snails. Whatever the reason, we had plenty of leafy beings looking none too leafy.

Later that day, while daydreaming of simpler Midwestern problems such as droughts and floods and landing the line-snapping catfish in my brother's pond, a solution snapped me back to L.A. reality, a semi-reality, if you will.

I remembered stalking my Ohio garden at night, flashlight in tow, capturing fish-worms for the next day's fishing expedition. Could I not similarly stalk this California garden, place the offending snails in a bucket, and cart them off to different feeding grounds? Indeed I could!

I explained the plan to Vicky—substituting "night crawlers" for "fish worms" (since Worms Are People Too.) She loved it! (However, when our worldly Aunt Lil said, "Oh, goody! Escargot!" Vicky's eyes flashed.)

I told her I would cart them down to the very typical (meaning bone dry) California streambed about 100 feet down the peaceful, secluded street.

As Vicky lounged and relaxed with a magazine that undoubtedly contained thought-provoking articles like "The Hidden Qualities of Mosquitoes" and "How to Sabotage the Perfect Mousetrap," I crept out with flashlight and pail and gently removed dozens of dining snails from our plants. When I had them all—a bucketful —I showed them to Vicky.

"How *cute,*" she said as she eyed an unoccupied fishbowl perched between an occupied fish tank and an occupied birdcage.

"Forget it kid!. No more pets!" Aunt Lil told her sternly.

As I carted the cute little sluggers down to the streambed, some crawled to the rim of the bucket and stretched their necks as if sight-seeing, reminiscent of vacationing kids poking their heads out of car windows. I emptied the bucket on a streambed-side boulder, the snails silently resenting the nonchalant abandonment. So not to appear insensitive, I picked them up and took them to some edible looking grass under a scrumptious-looking bush, a more suitable locale where they'd likely be safe from inhumane snail-predators, whatever *those* are.

"Goodbye, Slimy! So long, Poky! Farewell, Stretch!" I whispered to my favorite ones.

I then returned to Aunt Lil's where I slept the sleep of (if not a saint) at least that of a Midwestern hayseed who did well in the tricky world of California-style garden correctness.

Tales Taller than Sunflowers

Unfortunately, a quick peek at our garden the next morning showed that I had not captured them all. So I repeated the procedure that night and the next night, and the next . . . . It seemed like snails were dropping from the sky!

Then, while walking to the streambed on the sixth or seventh snail-liberation night, I looked more closely at the just-captured, sightseeing snails.

"What? Poky! Slimy! Stretch!" I cried, *my* eyes flashing.

We all went right back to the house; and Vicky's boyfriend, *his* eyes now flashing, drove us to another dry streambed on the *other side* of the hills.

Thus did our snail-liberation movement end. The teensy garden grew fabulously well. Unfortunately, I never got to test my gardening talents against earthquakes, mudslides *or* raging brush fires. Also, I—um—I—well—I sort of missed those pesky snails and our stirring moonlit walks.

As gardening season in Southern California reached full bloom, planting season in Ohio drew near. The time arrived for me to leave for another Midwestern gardening season, to a drought or to a flood, *or* (best of all) to weed forests and bean-eating bugs—a *good* season.

Moist-eyed Aunt Lil and my cousin Vicky said good-bye. I thanked Aunt Lil for the swell hospitality and for loaning me a nicotine patch whenever I ran out of smokes. I thanked Vicky for the equally swell hospitality and for the dog-eared copy of *Trap the Trappers.* They thanked me for my extended visit, their eyes flashing (or perhaps that was mere blinking) and bade me farewell.

Few life experiences are more relaxing and refreshing than helping a Leafy-Being Libber grow a totally correct, non-decorative California garden while operating an efficient and humane snail shuttle service on the side, except that of growing an Ohio produce garden where the only reason you'd visit with a flashlight at night is to collect fish worms. (But don't tell Vicky.)

CHAPTER TWO

The Garden of Lost Content
(Published in *Wyoming Rural Electric News*, Sept. 1991)

Once upon a spade, I was a business-like, purely pragmatic gardener. For example, I valued homegrown tomatoes as not only fresher and redder and tastier than store bought ones, but also as less expensive. I also felt healthily sure that my table fare included no unknown waxes or chemicals.

I think my current trouble began when I discussed my garden with several neighborhood kids the previous summer. The magic and mystery and poetry of growth crept into the otherwise scientific discourse. My objectivity crumbled like dry topsoil. As gardening evolved into something more than just another constructive hobby, the garden itself became a sort of sanctuary from an often harsh reality. Ultimately, I viewed my plants not as mere crops, but as individuals. And my garden as one big *happy* family!

This sprouted rapid-growth problems. I wound up tending to the garden way too personally. The plants grew attached to the soil and fell hopelessly in love with the growing season. Still, all things, including growing seasons, do eventually come to an end. While I felt somewhat melancholic at harvest time, my plants were downright devastated.

First, the peppers acted hot. The beets turned red and the mild-mannered zucchinis were steamed. Some of the tomatoes stewed for awhile, and the more expressive ones became saucy. The sensitive ones were crushed. And I left behind the spoiled ones, brats!

Visibly upset about the sudden termination of their fine little worlds, the pumpkins were all cut up, and although they suffered in silence, one by one the cabbages experienced broken hearts. The onions brought tears to *my* eyes! The lettuce and spinach wilted as the sunflowers ruefully hung their heads.

Like so many other forlorn victims of life, the broccoli simply gave up and went to seed, and the carrots dug right in and refused to leave, requiring me to use excessive force that was more characteristic of an insensitive brute than of a civilized gardener.

Tales Taller than Sunflowers

Only the green beans bravely faced their inescapable fate, but that *might* have been because they were too strung out to care.

Because of all of this, I have resolved to cultivate less sensitive vegetables. There will be no more soothing music, and *less* affectionate weeding and watering. There will be orderly, disciplined, non-nonsense rows. *This* summer I'll just talk to myself.

CHAPTER THREE

The Rust Of Us

Sometimes I wonder why I even grow green beans instead of buying them from Baron Van de Camp. Because of their shallow roots, they need watering more frequently than less fussy veggies. Because of their puny height, weeding and harvesting them gnarls one's backbone. Because of gourd-knows-what, bugs of every stripe and dot munch away at bean plants, leaving (or—*de*-leaving) their appearance looking something like moldy Swiss cheese plants.

They wind up looking awful, worse even than their gardener looks after a night spent doing the tango with his good ol' boy buddies, Jack Daniels and Johnny Walker.

To combat the appearance-destroying insects, I bring in fierce mercenaries, better known as toads, ladybugs and praying mantises.

Tales Taller than Sunflowers

I purchase these from enterprising nieces and nephews at bargain prices. As far as I know, however, these predatory carnivores just morph into vegetarians and *join* the bean-patch banquet in progress, because *my* bean plants become holier and holier as the summer progresses, and I *don't* mean in *any* religious sense.

I use other means to protect my green bean plants, but with no more success. I plant lovely and supposedly bug-repelling marigolds near the scruffy, bug-attracting green bean plants; and I sprinkle the little tramps with chili powder. This is all to no avail. The dining bugs *apparently* think the flowers are ambiance enhancing, and that the chili powder is an apt spice for their green cuisine. I *could* buy and use commercial insecticidal "dust," but the active ingredients in these have even *longer* names than the ingredients of artificial coffee creamer! (That which I won't put into my belly I won't put onto my veggies that wind up in that *same* belly.)

That's right! I am an *organic* gardener. I am furthermore a veggie rights activist. I am disturbed by the invegan method of lopping off heads of condemned cabbages and lettuces. I remember reading that the guillotined beneficiaries of the French Revolution, or at least their severed heads (including eyes and ears) *saw* the baskets as their heads plopped into them and *heard* the plops! Do we really want to use this inhumane French methods on our all

Tales Taller than Sunflowers

American gardens? Surely some gardening guru could devise a more compassionate execution method for condemned cabbages and lettuces? Perhaps we could use Leafal injections?

But let's get back to the bothersome green beans. I've been trying to disregard them, but lately they've posed another unattractive problem requiring my attention. It rained a persistently pesky drizzling rain for several days. The forecast arrogantly called for several more similarly soggy days. (*This* was really *not* a problem because of the ceaseless thirst of the shallow-rooted beans.) The *problem* was that time had arrived to *pick* those beans. And as *every* green bean grower knows, working in wet green bean plants will produce the bean peculiar problem called "rust," a fungus that looks like *hideous* splotches of rust. (I call it *hideous* even *knowing* I once tried to convince my would-be high-school sweetheart that my car's rust looked *cool*.) On the already haggish looking green bean leaves, rust turns bean rows into vegetative rust belts. Even *worse*, this rusty gunk spreads to the beans, rendering them *incredibly* inedible; but those green beans still needed picking!

I prefer baby beans, tender and mild. And some of my beans were approaching adolescence (a troubling time for any human's beans). Soon (due to their brutally short lifespan) the now babyish beans would grow old, dry, seedy, and tasteless! But if I plucked them now, it would *destroy* the already bedraggled plants and foredoom a couple generations of baby beans yet to otherwise *emerge!* So. . . because the plants were *already* bug-damaged. . . I *decided* to *sacrifice* them and to *satisfy* myself with one harvest of succulent baby beans!

My only problem, one I never before had to even consider, was whether by picking the baby beans wet, they would instantly develop rust. My gardening buddies didn't know either, *always* willing to give opinions when knowing nothing.

So I decided to call the local botanical experts, the Ohio State University's agricultural extension office. As I dialed I chuckled at the memory of a leftist history professor of mine at a Michigan university who once asked me why Ohioans were so conservative. I told her I thought it was related to Ohio's traditional farmland status, that those involved in growing things prefer predictability over uncertainty and the known over the unknown. What elicited my chuckle was the recollection of her response.

"Well, I thought that these days most farmers have doctorate degrees, and that would liberalize them."

Heh-heh—as *if* academia's liberalizing tentacles reached even into *their* agricultural departments, ha ha.

Little did I know . . .

Tales Taller than Sunflowers

They finally answered the phone. I spoke with an expert sounding woman named Dr Penenvy, if I remember it well (not that I often do).

I believe our communication problems began when (while describing the situation and my strategy) I used the term *baby beans*. Then a clearing of her throaty throat was closely followed by a frigid pause.

"Well, Sir," she said, "if I heard you *correctly*, you plan to save these unpicked *baby beans* at a hazard to the health of the *mother* plants."

(Now, when I hear the word *sir*, not to mention the word *mother*, I pay attention.)

"Have you considered the ethics of this?" she asked.

When I hear the word *ethics* instead of the word *morals*, I usually stand back among earthy planetary citizens like my peppers and reconsider the consideration.

"Well," I stammered, "the mother—the plants, they aren't much use to me, at least not anymore. I'd be happy just to save *this* particular batch of baby beans!"

"And in so doing," she replied in a hopelessly authoritative tone, "you would willingly *destroy* the mother plants?"

"Um," I considered (and this was a hard one) "yes, madam.'

Tales Taller than Sunflowers

"A typically patriarchal attitude," she snapped; and she clicked-off (as in smacked down) her phone without answering my question!

I never even got to tell her I was *actually* a pro-choice gardener and *not* a patriarch, for Moses' sake. I pick my veggies when I choose, and I had chosen *now*. (Incidentally, the "mother" plants did not just rust away, and the baby beans? Well, they were tender and mild, just like I like them!)

Afterwards, I got on university's website—just a hunch. I found Dr. Penenvy's listing and found out that before her master's and doctorate degrees in agricultural science, she had earned a bachelor's (or is that a *bachelorette's*?) in botany with a minor in *women's* studies.

So beware when discoursing freely (or otherwise) with a feminist farmer. Avoid gender issues! (Don't tell her you'd like to plow her field.) As for me, the next time I need gardening advice I'll avoid academia entirely and ask an earthy old gardener like my neighbor Nick who has the education of a half-century of digging in wisdom-bestowing dirt.

CHAPTER FOUR

The Homeless Gardeners

Although we often hear about the plight of the homeless, I am pleased to now announce newly established rights of the homeless—homeless *gardeners,* that is. Like a promising seedling out of the earth, the welcome news emerged out of Boulder, Colorado. There a gardening couple successfully claimed "squatter's rights" to a portion of a large, pricey, otherwise vacant lot where they had not only planted and tended a garden, but where they had also stacked firewood and thrown parties—my kind of gardeners!

The owners of the lot (valued by them at a cool million) testified that they had often walked their dog past the lot, but they had never noticed a thing.

Tales Taller than Sunflowers

I say, thank goodness they only walked their dog *past*—and not *through*—the covert garden. I add that if they failed to notice a fine, thriving garden on their own land, not to mention possibly a blazing fire and rousing party garden-side, then they are obviously not gardeners—in which case, they deserve no rights!

The judge agreed with me—or, chronologically speaking, I agreed with him ("Your Honor"). In granting the homeless gardeners one-third of the lot, the judge noted the (formerly) homeless gardeners exhibited an attachment to the land that was "Stronger than the true owners' attachment." *Yes, Your Honor, gardeners always do.* This Solomon-like judge was, bless his soil, obviously a green thumber.

The applicable property law is called adverse possession." Every state has some version of it, and the elements may differ from state to state. Basically, the elements of "adverse possession" are that possession of the real estate is actual, open, notorious, exclusive, hostile, under cover of claim or right, and continuous and uninterrupted for the statutory period. So, homeless gardeners everywhere in the U.S. can cultivate hope, as long as they meet the requirements of the laws of their state. As for home owning gardeners, you deserve rights too; and by gardening your land and therefore using it, you protect those rights, just *don't* quit! Keep the green faith, your garden, *and* your land.

Tales Taller than Sunflowers

Now, as a skeptic you doubt the existence of "homeless gardeners" right? That does not jive with your image of the typical homeless person. Well, those persons are *gardenless* as well as homeless, *doubly* unfortunate. Of course there are always gardenless homeowners. And therefore there exists the opposite, namely homeless gardeners who merely cherish a *different* type of green. And wholesome, well-rounded gardening homeowners cherish b*oth* greens, gardens *and* spendable green.

Think All American Johnny Appleseed types, rootless even as they scatter seeds that sprout roots. Newspaper *Home & Garden* sections should divide into two sections. (Gardening homeowners can read both sections,) Home would be one section. Garden would be another section, because you *can* have one without the other. Furthermore, as for me, I'd much rather be a homeless gardener, than a gardenless homeowner.

And I am (as of late) a kind of homeless gardener, albeit no longer a *hopeless* gardener, if you catch my drift. You see, for three of the last four seasons I have been an apartment dweller, and there's no place for a garden in an apartment. (In these times, my landlord should probably be thankful for that.) My apartment building sits precariously near the campus where I've attended college for, let's just say, "quite awhile." Call me a *gradual* student.

Indeed, I could probably claim squatter's rights to that campus, showing a "stronger attachment" than those under-gradual students who rush through in the minimum four years as if college was a rats' race awaiting them. What makes me like school so much that I linger longer? Well, it ain't the learnin'! No, it's the pleasure of living among incredibly frenzied young party animals during the non-gardening seasons; and then having the gardening season off, academically speaking.

That's when I grow my garden at my parents' place. I probably have, I now know, a *legal* claim to the garden there. With purposefully ominous undertones, I mentioned the Colorado case to non-gardening Pops, who used to grow weeds where my garden now lay, and before calling his legal adviser, he mounted a tentative defense.

"I'm strongly attached to that garden, too!"

"No, you're strongly attached to the tasty, nutritious, *free* veggies that come from out there," I retorted.

"Well, don't you remember when I bought gas for the rototiller you bought?"

"I'm still listening."

"Don't you remember when I spread wood ash on it? That's good for *our* garden!" He said as he righteously stomped off toward the phone where I soon overheard him speaking in choked tones.

Tales Taller than Sunflowers

(I wondered if I could fill the legal elements of the cause of action for adverse possession in *my* state. . . *probably not*. Maybe I should call *my* legal advisor.)

I remembered the wood ash from the brick barbeque pit standing deliciously near my garden. Sometimes when I was off gradually getting through yet another endless semester, Pops burned gourd-knows-what kind of trash in the pit, and then got rid of the resultant mess by spreading it in my garden. Then he expected gratitude (or at least compliments) for this act of desecration! For days after I returned from campus I collected bolts, nuts (*not* the edible kind) rusty door-hinges and ashy strips of fossilized paint from my garden.

Once, after discovering that I had secretively borrowed a good portion of the contents of the wine cellar, he threatened to plow my garden under. That's right! I and my innocent veggie kids suffered serious verbal abuse (which we drowned out with some more pilfered wine that night).

Anyway, back to that Colorado case. It seems some homeowners (probably non-gardening ones) in Boulder reacted strongly to the court ruling, and picketed (and I don't mean a pleasant little white fence). They probably trampled the veggie plants in the process, the brutes! The irate non-gardeners (I'm *almost* certain they are) even started Internet blogs which they filled with fury, most likely (in the meantime) neglecting their own property.

As I said, there are two *different* types of green pursued by two *different* types of people. Then again, there is now that more recent, *third* type of green. Speaking of which, I was over at my environmentalist cousin's the other day describing the Colorado case when suddenly his eyes grew wide and greenish saliva formed at his lip-corners.

"Look, cousin," he babbled, "You *must* admit that environmentalists exhibit the *strongest* attachment to the whole planet."

"You mean the *environmentalists* shall inherit the earth?" I asked.

"Well, it looks like we don't *need* to wait to inherit with these newly established legal rights!" he foolishly concluded.

As I gazed across his gardenless backyard (he's always too busy on the internet and the Discovery Channel) I suggested, "Why don't you go spread the news on some of the major environmental blogs?"

As he excitedly headed inside to do just that, I called after him, "AND TELL YOUR E-BUDDIES THAT WE NORTHERN GARDENERS ARE STILL IMPATIENTLY WAITING FOR THE GLOBAL WARMING THEY PROMISED US!"

Once he was inside, I located a hoe and shovel in his garage and went to stake my claim (later, *my* tomatoes) to a moderate portion of *his* sprawling backyard.

Good old Henry David Thoreau, a homeless gardener until he built his cabin by Walden Pond, said to build castles in the air. With all due respect to him, I say, "Build them in the dirt."

CHAPTER FIVE

Gender Bended Pests Could Create Bedlam

I've tried every conceivable weapon against garden insect pests, both nastily unnatural pesticides and wholly wholesome organic methods, but now some mad genius has conceived the inconceivable—a gender-bending insect powder that would make even the Hollyweird crowd perversely proud.

This new weapon comes not from the west coast, but from across the ocean, from gay and merry old England. From England it's spreading all over Europe, like a plague for bad bugs. It's called "Esosex" and is manufactured by a company called "Exosect." Presumably they did not want the word *sex* in the company name, because that would bring too many late night calls from weirdo's (not me) looking for a good time. Esosex is a trap that lures unsuspecting male insects into a box-like trap containing female pheromone powder that coats them. Once outside they attract other guy insects with the mating urge and boy (or girl) aren't *both* parties surprised at what happens next!

Needless to say, these close encounters of the homosectual kind not only lead to insect fighting, but they also *do not* lead to baby insects! So who *cares* if cross-dressing aphids and Japanese beetles become sexually confused? The gay-guy insects suffer, and the women insects wonder where all the real men went; and to tell you the truth, the only insect pests I would *not* wish to suffer such fates are mosquitoes! (After all, right now only female skeeters suck blood, but if male skeeters start exhibiting a feminine side, then our mosquito problem would be roughly doubled.)

Another potential problem with this fantastic new weapon against pests is *transferability*. Because one of the reasons this stuff works so well is when an unsuspecting guy insect embraces a powdered transvestite insect (thinking that he is a she) then it also gets powdered—*feminized*—and becomes *another* sexual magnet to other horny guy insects, so on and so forth. What if this powdered sexual confusion gets transferred outside the wretched family of insect pests? Consider the *helper* insects, gardeners' friends. The gender bending would be okay among honeybees; the males ("drones") who do not now work in our gardens or anywhere else, when feminized would presumably help out with pollination chores. As for ladybugs, I don't see much trouble there, either. After all, a dude ladybug is already a *ladybug!*

What I worry about are those maniacal pest-devouring praying mantises. Their very straightforward, heretofore heterosexual mating habits involve the insatiable female calmly biting off the head of the male shortly after. . . um. . . *you know.* Maybe the dude ought to offer her a post-coitus smoke—maybe that would appease her. Then again, maybe man mantises are lousy in bed. What happens when an un-powdered manly mantis tries to mate with a powdered (unmanly) mantis? Does the feminized mantis then complete the traditional head-chomping ritual, or merely kick the other's butt? Or, when the powder rubs off on the yet masculine mantis, feminizing it, do they then simultaneously attempt to bite off each other's heads, or simply smoke and chitchat? I suspect that with all this mating confusion they'll have little energy left with which to attack and destroy insect *pests*. Maybe this *horrific* scenario is what they've been praying *against* all these years.

And what if all these depraved insects accidentally powder our veggie plants? I would anticipate bedlam amongst the tomatoes! The Better Boys would morph into Better *Girls*, which I guess would be okay. The Beef Masters, however, would become Beef

Tales Taller than Sunflowers

Mistresses, dangerous if too hefty and heavy-handed. Plus—the Early Girls would be left with no one with whom to flirt, but on the other vine, they'd have more tomatoes with which to exchange juicy gossip.

And what if their concerned gardeners get the nefarious powder on themselves? All of a sudden, all of the dude veggie gardeners would start growing flowers and herbs. En masse they'd start joining gardening clubs! Can you imagine a newly feminized, yet pot bellied dude gardener hosting a garden-club meeting? All of the *real* lady gardeners would feel mighty uncomfortable among "his" drill presses and table saws, crushed beer cans and girly calendars. Instead of the usual refreshments—dainty club sandwiches and tea—he-she would serve fat, greasy cheeseburgers and pass around cans of warm beer with which to wash them down.

As for myself, I aim to keep the devious powder off of me and *away* from my sexually *straight* garden. It is true that my girl Maria sometimes (okay—*often*) prefers her girlfriends' company to mine, but I just can't imagine being one of the girls. I also *refuse* to wear her clothes no matter how often she asks me wear them. The sunbonnets that look so lovely on her would look *ridiculous* on me. Furthermore, I would never want to walk like she does, because I would throw out a hip!

Therefore, with growing season rapidly approaching, I'll figure out a traditional *American* way to battle insect pests—namely, manly praying mantises and non-ladylike ladybugs, as well as their partners of the *opposite* gender.

I am thankful for such goodies as Swiss cheese, Danish pastries, Swedish meatballs, Italian ices, French bread and French fries, Italian dressing and Italian sausages, and (especially) Irish and German beers. Many European eats and drinks are A-okay with me; however, when it comes to gardening, we don't need *any* new twists from the old world.

CHAPTER SIX

Botanical Correctness Could Branch Inward

When it comes to branching, gardeners usually think of stuff branching *outward*. We are (of course) thinking of *natural* stuff. However, some stuff (and some guff) are not only *un*natural, but it *must* branch inward, because it starts on the West Coast and spreads our earthly way from there—movies and political correctness for example. Midwestern gardeners typically don't care much for political *anything*, except for (perhaps) around election time, which comes in the otherwise dull off-season. Furthermore, "political" and "correctness" seem a contradiction of terms.

It is time to beware. The West Coast is sprouting the concept of *botanical* correctness. It will *surely* branch our way, like ingrown toenails or mutant poison ivy or something similarly irritating. An

Tales Taller than Sunflowers

ill wind blew me news of California's so-called PlantRight campaign that, with the help of government agencies and other infamous actors, seeks to "empower, meaning persuade, I think. (Although whether this persuasion is through brainwashing or simple torture is unclear.) Yes! California gardeners plant right! And planting right in this case means to not plant certain "invasive" (illegal immiplants) plants that allegedly threaten California's wetlands and wildlife.

In my part of the country the problem is protecting plants from invasive wildlife, and not invasive plant life! What style of kick-butt plant exists out there that could "threaten" the likes of coyotes, cougars and scorpions?

One of the PlantRight campaign primary targets is a giant reed called Arundo Donax. (Did you notice the suspiciously foreign name?) According to the paranoid PlantRight freaks, this ruthless plant crowds out *native* plants, which I assume, means cacti as well as palm, citrus and redwood trees. I can't help but to feel a tad skeptical about claims the giant *reed* could crowd out a *giant* tree! Arundo also supposedly threatens native wildlife with habitat change. Is this a parallel to California's illegal immigrant paranoia? Do these plants really come to California to threaten native wildlife? Does this occur late at night and involve unbelievable levels of perversion and debauchery? Plants better watch out for those

California voter referendums, government regulations, increased border patrols, and vigilante squads!

The giant reed stands accused of aiding and abetting wildfires. (It seems like *everything* in California is doggone wild.) Whether it also played a role in the recent string of LA bank robberies has not yet been established, but detectives are undoubtedly looking into it.

Getting away from Californian defenses against invading threats to their wild lifestyles, and getting back to the concept of botanical correctness, one must note it is not like Ohio is in the Middle Ages regarding this fantastic concept. Take the case of the gargantuan Ohio chemical company, Scotts. Scotts makes the wildly popular fertilizer-mix, Miracle-Grow® or is it Gro®? (Either they or I do not spell it rite.) You have probably used, or have seen somebody use the bright blue powder. My question about its blueness is what type of coloring got it that way? With the ingredients *in* Miracle-Grow® (or -Gro®) it would more likely be colored a less appealing blend of purple and orange and chartreuse if displaying its natural color. Scotts has been complying with these botanically correct times by offering *organic* garden fertilizers colored a less appealing, but a more natural color than the chemical-blue of Miracle-Grow® (or Gro®). Furthermore, they may even exceed California in mixing political with botanical correctness. A couple of years ago, they not only banned employees from smoking at their headquarters, but they banned them from smoking *anywhere*, including in their very own homes and gardens, or risk being fired!

Apparently this amazing edict was approved by their Fuehrer, I mean their CEO (Chief Executioner Oaf). I understand not allowing smoking at explosive chemical plants, but in private homes and gardens? Have they not heard gardening lessens (that's right) the chance of lung cancer? Or are they (like certain Californians) more concerned with running other peoples' lives than with other peoples' health? While PlantRight tells people what not to grow in their gardens, Scotts tells people what not to do in their homes or gardens or anywhere else. If I worked for Scotts I would tell them to take the job and shovel it. A puff of a cigarette harms you far less than a swallow of Miracle-Grow® (or -Gro®) which (incidentally) contains chemicals that can and have been used to make bombs!

I'm not concerned about Scotts. They're in my own backyard, and in my own backyard I (unlike their employees) decide what grows and what goes. However, for several weeks after hearing about PlantRight I kept peering over my shoulder as I sat near my garden at night enjoying the fragrance of freshly tuned soil. I feared not invasive plants, but invasive nonsense from a wild westerly direction. I will *not* have California telling *me* how or what to plant. (I am thinking about growing tobacco this year, just for the *na-na-na-nana* of it.)

I have now quit fretting. If the sturdy, ancient, deep-rooted redwoods can't branch this far, then how could the flimsy, flighty, shallow-rooted idea of botanical correctness?

CHAPTER SEVEN

On Homo-Herbal Relationships

Loosen Up that Dirt a Little and Relieve Tree Stress advised the Home-and-Garden newspaper section heading. Although I am a farmer of vegetables and *not* trees, this captured my attention and aroused long buried emotional distress. The article discussed philosophically stimulating strategies such as deep core aeration and vertical mulching. However, I was most intrigued by the "Stress" component of the article. Apparently, trees possess personality and as in vegetable plants, these personalities can become unstable, unpredictable, irritable and irritating! (And I thought these more settled and mature members of the plant queendom could quell such neurotic, hypersensitive character traits!)

Tales Taller than Sunflowers

I sympathize with hand-wringing tree-farmers. My vegetable plants also develop occasional psychological problems, thus causing *me* problems and twisting our formerly stable relationship into a sort of love-hate affair. They sometimes bother me with their exaggerated stress anxieties. The broccoli is stressed by heat, the eggplant by cold, and the beans are stressed by everything betwixt and between the two extremes. They do not manage stress very well; however, their alleged stress is actually one of my lesser concerns. (Counseling usually solves that!) What troubles me most deeply about them is flirtation, infidelity, lack of true commitment and ultimately desertion!

When younger and dumber, I tried about everything to salvage our relationships, from the latest scientific horticultural techniques to the most innovative garden-design artistry, to the strongest shows of care and affection imaginable. Today (as self-protection) I practice emotional distancing. I believe by avoiding too much intimacy and attachment I can avoid feelings of betrayal and rejection later.

I also attempt to avoid the excesses and extremes of my gardening neighbors. Nick coddles and pampers and undoubtedly spoils his veggie-partners with slavishly adhered-to watering schedules, four types of nutritional supplements, extraordinary weed-eradication efforts, and mulching so extravagant as to make me sick! (I recently installed a shrubbery barrier between his garden and mine to protect my covetous veggie-partners from jealousy pangs.) Nick's plants seem quite fond of him, but I suffer no envy. Sometimes when I peer over the shrubbery I observe Nick pacing and muttering. I believe he is questioning their sincerity, wondering if the only reason that they to like him so much is because *he* likes *them* so much. Doris unemotionally tosses seeds and seedlings into ordinary soil and nonchalantly tosses down forlorn leaves as mulch, later letting her veggie-partners fend for themselves. Although hardly a one-month stand, theirs is a casual relationship devoid of binding ties. Expecting little in return, she gets just that. Perhaps she could be a little closer, but who is to judge? She may be protecting herself, because she was formerly severely hurt—heartbroken! —in some forlorn summer past.

I have learned to tread the middle ground between these two extremes. I give my heart, but not my soul, at least not *all* of it! In return I expect honnesty and respect, but not necessarily long term commitment.

I get back what I put into it. Their appearances are lovely. I am proud to be seen with them. They are receptive and responsive to my advances and they aren't cold fishes or veg-fatales. They flourish and flower and make the honeybees hum. My heart melts away! They eventually reciprocate my many favors by bestowing me with colorful tasty gifts. This is *not* a one-way relationship.

With that said, let me confess our relationship, although *not* one-way, is ultimately poisoned and doomed by incompatibilities. I am less a romanticist and more a realist and certain troubling realities have hardened my heart. Some plants are mighty flirtatious, namely peppers and squash, blossoming far more than they can possibly give. They are also moody. Sometimes they want my sprinkles, sometimes they don't. Sometimes they act wilted, other times elated. I' have long suspected them of infidelity. Last week I (finally) obtained irrefutable evidence. Neighbor Nick, long known to me as lustful regarding vege-beings, brazenly reached out and sensuously plucked one of my more erotic pepper plant's admittedly enticing yet spoken-for fruits. I rather expected her—or *it* (I don't know anymore) to react with indignant anger or at least maidenly dismay, perhaps even a leafy slap to Nick's kindly but lecherous face. Instead, the plant in question merrily swayed in the sumptuous breeze wiggling her lush peppers in a most scintillating manner—the floozy! Where was the modesty? Where was the loyalty? Where was the commitment? None exists. No longer a fool in gloves, I have finally accepted this. Although I wandered about zombie-like for a while, now I am better. I am "well adjusted." Next time they desert me upon the arrival of October's chill winds, I shall grind no teeth, suffer no grief, plague myself not with self-interrogations as to where I went wrong. Ignoring time tested common sense guidelines for healthy homo-herbal relationships, I gave too much of myself and expected too much in return.

So to all you tree-lovers fretting about "stressed" trees, I ask, "Is that any reason to cry?" Do you not know what most of us have already learned through hard experience? Those who selfishly whine and complain about stress tend to *cause* more stress than they themselves suffer. Such whining is often a thinly veiled effort to gain attention. I have now cancelled plans to plant a small fruit orchard. Any more close encounters with deep-rooted neurotics would surely drive me over the hedge.

It appears all members of the leafy persuasion are alike. Don't take them so seriously. Take them with a grain of salt (and possibly some pepper when dealing with potatoes). Pluck and run! Be you a tree-farmer, a vegetable farmer, a farmer of vines, roots, buds, bushes, flowers or trees, do not be a vulnerable farmer of hearts. It is a doomed pursuit that will leave you groveling in the dirt.

CHAPTER EIGHT

My Most Irreligious Gardening Partners

After whipping up some glorious tuna salad thick with Miracle Whip, and after whispering a reverently lengthy pre-meal prayer, my mother sat to lunch with me. She was especially interested in the garden I planted and now tended for her. After polishing off the sandwich and while answering her gentle inquiries, I thought it a fine time to suggest a glass of the only booze in the house, Christian Brothers brandy.

She demurred and continued with her questions.

"Have you continued to use plenty of *Miracle Gro* on it?" she asked.

My mother prefers products with names blessed by words like *miracle* and *Christian* because she expects them to produce miraculous or at least Christianly results. Her tuna sandwiches taste heavenly, and the brandy makes me feel downright spiritual at times. But I prefer *organic* gardening, fish emulsion, bone meal and compost to *Miracle Gro:* and I told her so.

Detecting the beginnings of hurt feelings in her saintly eyes, I quickly added, "Oh, but mom, the plants have grown fabulously well! Their only real problem comes from *insects*. The beans and cabbage and eggplants, for example, look mighty holey."

Boy, did her eyes brighten at that! Soon she grasped my meaning and reverently poured us two glasses (one of them tall) of *Christian Brothers'* finest.

Sipping, I wondered aloud whether there might exist something like *Miracle Bug Remover*.

"No dear—I checked. Anyway, I thought you preferred *organic* gardening," she said.

"Yea, sure—but I also prefer veggies with fewer holes than sponges have."

"Well, Doris told me just the other day that her grandson found some sort of large cocoon earlier this spring and kept it a sealed aquarium, and that now it has hatched, guess what it hatched?"

"Butterflies?" I asked, staring into my near-empty glass, wondering where all of this would lead.

Tales Taller than Sunflowers

"No. Praying mantises!" she said as her eyes brightened again, and stayed that way. "I hear that they're good for gardens. They eat the bad bugs."

She meant the bad ones were the non-praying ones, I suppose. I too had heard these devout carnivorous bugs helped gardeners by eating the irreverent vegetarian bugs. After a perhaps premature celebratory refill of the brandy, I trotted over to neighbor Doris' house, to talk with her imp grandson who was summering with her.

He proudly showed me his aquarium. It held what looked like hundreds of tiny mantises, a crusade-worthy army of them! I offered five bucks for the whole blessed batch.

"Cool—that's how much I need to buy Billy's piranha!" he said. "Plus, they'll sure eat lots of your mom's garden's bugs. I didn't know *what* to feed them. Some of them must have got so hungry that they escaped, although I don't know how. There were twice as many yesterday!

I tried reducing my offer to two-fifty, but he had to have that piranha. So, I forked over the money and carted off the reduced forces to mother's sacred yet buggy garden, scattering twenty or thirty here, fifty or sixty there.

"Get to work, you saints," I encouraged.

Tales Taller than Sunflowers

They disappeared into the holey greenery. In fact, I never could find *any* after that. I figured they were succeeding, because the veggie-leaf holes decreased to thousands instead of millions. And when strolling through that garden at night, with some soul-warming brandy in hand, I swear I sometimes heard faint sounds of fierce battles, *massacres* taking place amidst the dark green.

Thinking I might learn something about these devout insects and thus better utilize their divine powers, I sought information on them. Bit by bit I realized I might have unwittingly made a deal with devils (not the imp—the insects).

For example, I found out why their population had halved in the aquarium. It seems if baby praying mantises hatch in an enclosure and have no other food they turn on each other, turn and turn and turn until only two well fed babies are left. Then one eats the other. What kind of baby food is that? Maybe *that's* why mantises learn to pray so young. They learn to pray their stronger siblings have plenty to eat!

I also found out adult mantises have been observed seizing and eating not just bugs, but other creatures, small garter snakes and *humming birds*. Mother had a hummingbird feeder near her garden, and earlier in the summer I'd occasionally watch a humming bird using it. Lately, however, I had seen any. I started feeling mighty suspicious about these imposter prayers, these hummingbird molesters. Praying—ha! I began to doubt that they even had souls, began to think that "*preying* monsters" would make a more fitting name for them.

But worst of all were their sexual ethics. After they you know what, the female bites the head off of her mate, instead of allowing him a quick nap. How romantic is that? Does she say a quick pre-meal prayer first? To whom? We know where the babies get their eating habits, from Mother Mantis. They were quite unlike my own *sincerely* prayerful mother, who probably wouldn't bite the head off of a chocolate bear. I no longer asked my girlfriend Maria to visit my mom's garden with me. Other females, especially the assertive ones, far too easily influence her.

Then Doris' imp grandson came over and told me that "somebody killed" his pet piranha. I *knew* who did it—those atheistic she-wolves in nuns' clothing, that's who! It probably happened during a sacrificial black mass. All this didn't bother me for long, though. When giant leather-clad mantis-chicks started visiting my dreams grasping bibles in one hand and clasping sadomasochistic gear in the other, I knew I had to stop studying and obsessing about these heretical insecticidal maniacs, and just appreciate the debugged veggies.

I'm fine now—me, and the *Christian Brothers* too. Plus, at least my mother never needs to pray anymore for deliverance from biblical-proportioned plagues of veggie-eating bugs. Instead, I suppose she prays for the rehabilitation and salvation of those would be garden saints.

CHAPTER NINE

The Chives, They Ain't A-Changin'

Usually I skim over newspapers' *Home & Garden* sections. Sure, I always *welcome* garden-related information and insights, but *those* Home & Garden headings are a tad misleading. *"Home and a Very Occasional Smidge Of Brief Gardening Tips If You're Lucky!"* seems a far more accurate title of the content. I intuit that the phenomenon is somehow linked to the sparseness of garden-related ads in relation to the great glut of real estate ads, but peering too deeply into such phenomena always makes me feel queasy.

I recently spotted a full-length *gardening* article and gleefully pounced on it! Nevermind that its heading had slightly troubling implications—something like *"Seeds That Keep Pace With Changing Lifestyles."* Overjoyed nonetheless at finally finding some green literature among all the bad news, I shoved skepticism into my mind's backroom, ordered it to stay there, and eagerly read paragraph one about "Royal Chantenay Carrots" and "Purple Ruffles Basil." Then an "Oh oh" drifted out of my mind's backroom into its front room, accompanied by triumphantly grinning skepticism. In paragraph two, I learned, *"Regarding Vegetables, Appropriateness of Name is Important."*

"How thoroughly charming!" I thought and I asked my straight shooting hot peppers what they thought of this imaginative concept.

"Fine," they pleasantly responded and then added, "So long as we can appropriately name the gardeners."

"Go ahead," I diplomatically agreed, anticipating something appropriately complimentary if not downright reverent.

"Sheep!" they cried out, nearly collapsing in laughter. As I hurried off, I heard them continue, "Baaa! *Baaaaa!*"

"So much for narrow-minded vegetables!" I thought.

I shut out their derisive voices and skepticism's front room finger-tapping, and resumed reading the timely article. Soon I was privy to a seed company executive's stimulating theory that *American Gardens Have Shrunk "Both in Time and Space."* (Time *and* space?) The executive apparently then rushed off before any sharp reporters could ask him where seedless grapes come from and, more importantly, where they might be headed.

Since neither he nor Albert Einstein is available to further explain this time-and-space relationship, I humbly will. Trendy gardeners' backyards are so crammed with hot tubs and redwood decks and other impressively expensive stuff, that garden space back has shriveled and shrunk. Furthermore, to pay for the impressively expensive stuff, not to mention fashionable produce, they must waste vast quantities of that most precious resource, time, rushing about making more and more and more money, thus shrinking their gardening time. So you see it takes no genius, no Albert Einstein, and certainly no Seed Company Executive to understand the concept.

On to the next informative, subtly lyrical paragraph where *"User Friendly Plants"* are discussed without even gagging. What talent! I suspect whoever coined that term (probably just another genius flirting with madness) was alluding to and was likely influenced by such *user-friendly* cash crops as marijuana or opium poppies. (I hope that they exercise sufficient restraint, because those plants are also *abuser* friendly.)

"Designer Produce" was mentioned next, and practically in the same breath with a straight face. I just knew they'd stop at designer fertilizer. (Smell is a key factor in taste. Bad smell and good taste *cannot* tango together.)

Tales Taller than Sunflowers

Suddenly it struck me this article was not aimed at the likes of simple old unsophisticated me, but at the hip-yupster constituency, those rare individualists who number in the millions. The front of my mind, fully furnished and brilliantly redecorated by the artist skepticism, pointed out despite all the media attention, the Yupsters have not saved the rain forests as they promised. (But they did sell a lot of movies and tee shirts!)

I wondered if second-hand fragrance restrictions and mandatory seed-belt laws would soon be enacted into law out of a deeply felt personal concern for the broccoli crowd's health and welfare? I mentioned this to my broccoli, and they *seemed* to counter-propose "air bags." However, upon a closer listen, I realized it was a counter-charge of "wind-bags!"

As to the seemingly inevitable Mandatory Bug Testing, I have mixed feelings. I am generally against inevitable, against mandatory, *and* against testing, but am also against bugs—despite Insect Rights Groups' warnings—and have indeed waged my own moderately successful War on Bugs. I would perhaps welcome the yupsters' aid in the worthy endeavor, but I fear my post-war garden will then include certain war-refugees, namely *Designer Bugs*, too stylish and expensive and well-bred to simply smoosh.

But let's get back to the exceedingly enlightening article, because weeks might pass before I see another like it!

Tales Taller than Sunflowers

I learned that an estimable British grocery chain is, in trend-setting manner, claiming exclusive marketing rights to a specially developed, finely educated, purebred tomato named *Melrow*. (Why not *Sir Philip* or *Liz Beth*?) This tomato is presumably neither a fruit nor a vegetable but a guru or something else. Indeed, its developer, a British plant breeder, reportedly has a personal relationship with the Supreme Bean. Both the breeder and the tomato anticipate reincarnation as sushi, caviar or bottled water.

As for me, I absolutely refuse to raise any snobs in my earthy garden. Why would I trade wholesome, generous Better Boys for shallow, self-absorbed "Melrow" types? The next thing you know, I'd need a membership card and formal attire merely to gain admittance to my own garden!

The grammatically correct article also touched upon, if not actually caressed *"The Importance of the Environment."* (The environment is *important*? Surely they jest! I would never have guessed without guidance.) Although I appreciated the generous sharing of this strange new fact, I also resented the fact the article inconsistently failed to discuss how we might impress people and increase income through our monopoly of this.

Not only is the environment—*gasp!* —important, but the brilliant breeder of the snobbish tomatoes prophesizes that "Americans will soon be clamoring for produce by name." Let's fool them (wink-wink). While the yupsters take the names, we'll take the produce. That way they'll impress their peers and fool themselves, and we'll impress our tummies and fool nobody.

Finally, I learned *"Gardening's Biggest Competitor is The Super Market."*

So *that* was the article's main point. We already knew that! I mean, every last intrinsically good and natural and wholesome human activity must eventually contend with "The Super Market." Regardless of that common knowledge, the article supported its main point with rich details and fresh examples and significant quotes. Furthermore, it was truly news I could use. Yes, I shoveled it into my compost heap!

Out of fear I contaminated my garden by bringing the news so near, the next day, I questioned my chives: "So, are ya'all goin' pro-choice on me or *what?*"

"We're basically just pro-you calming down and shutting up and doing a little weeding 'round here," they snapped back.

See what I mean? Those up-from-earth veggie plants, they keep me healthy and happy and sane.

CHAPTER TEN

Militant Honeybees Boycott Garden

Babysitting my garden-wrecking nieces and nephews one night, long after they were dreaming the dreams of youth, I furtively crept up to their movie collection. I sought one of my favorite old classics, *The Jungle Book* or *The Wizard of Oz*, but could not find either. Then I remembered the kids and I had worn them out from repeated viewings, sometimes at *their* insistence, other times at mine. So, looking for something new and unusual, I ran across something entitled *Bee Movie*.

Naturally, I'm a big fan of bees—they buzz so sweetly as they pollinate my veggies' blossoms—I decided to watch this. The general storyline, in case you have not seen it, goes like this. A young worker bee who does not love working discovers that humans have been stealing bees' honey, and he recovers it in a lawsuit, becoming famous and leisure-classed as a result; *but*—in case you have not seen it, I ought not spoil the rest for you.

Movie watching is for the summer night. Gardening is for the summer day. However, when I visited my lush plot the next day, it seemed eerily silent. I soon found out why. Instead of buzzing busily about, the local honeybees lounged lazily about on my garden bench, some of them sleepily sipping the remains of a cup of soda. They all seemed so lethargic that I thought maybe it was not soda, but leftover beer in that cup—bees are not averse to alcohol, in case you've ever seen them buzzing erratically around fallen, half-fermented fruit. Looking closer, *nope.* I don't drink red beer, at least not knowingly.

I thought I was perhaps still under the influence of the *Bee Movie*. But I found out instead that those honeybees were possibly under the influence of some militant socialist arm of the feminist movement.

I muttered to myself, "Are you bees gaining vengeance for humans stealing your honey by stealing our sugary beverages as reparations?"

It startled me to then hear a buzzfully derisive reply, "Nope—we're on strike, mister."

After getting over my shock, I stuttered "What? Do you guys mean you're boycotting my garden?"

"*Girl*-cotting it, sister, and we're not *guys* either."

"Of course!" I quickly agreed. "You're *bees*."

"We're *Girl* bees. And that is *exactly* why we're on strike."

That was when I realized missionary feminist preachers had gotten hold of those bees. They have many times mistaken men for insects. Perhaps they had now also mistaken these insects for women.

"Hey, I'm not such a bad dude," I protested. "I treat my own girl with the utmost respect (I did not add 'or else')."

"That's none of *our* beeswax," one of them buzzed. "What we're furious about are boy bees."

Whew—so it was nothing personal against me.

Attempting to let them know I was not unfamiliar with boy bee antics, I said, "Yeah, I know. Just last night I watched a movie where a boy worker bee had the audacity to file suit against the human race!"

The buzzing merriment that greeted this statement made me smile.

"Yep, some nerve, eh? Pretty damn funny, I agree!"

"Oh, we're not laughing at that lawsuit business," one of them buzzed. "It's the idea of a boy bee being a *worker*."

"Why—what's so funny about *that*?" I asked. "Lots of worker bees were boys in that movie."

"Ha-ha, buzz-buzz. If you believe everything you see and hear in movies, you're not even worth talking to [Funny, but my girlfriend Maria has told me that, too.] In the *real* world, boy bees—we call them drones—do absolutely *no* work."

"Pretty lazy, huh?" I diplomatically asked.

"Damn right—they're worthless, no-account chiselers! We girls get stuck with *all* the work. That's why we're on strike."

"Look girls," I said, seeking to strike a bargain. "I can feel your pain. My own sister was once married to a drone. I would've punched him in the nose if I could've reached it. But I am a decent guy. I even cook for my girl sometimes, and I do the dishes afterwards (I again did not add 'or else'). Look, if you'd at least work in my garden—just smell those swell blossoms—I'll bring you all the sugary beverages you want, as well as honey, which rightfully belongs to you anyway. Heck, I'll even bring out some fermented fruit juices, and we can party—get on a good buzz! And I won't bring a drop for those disgraceful drones! What do you say, honeys?" I thought, "*There*, that ought to do it."

Once again I thought wrong. The bees, many of whom had yawned throughout my lengthy, impassioned proposal, advised me to "Buzz off," and promptly fell asleep.

Tales Taller than Sunflowers

Then I woke up—to the buzz of a fuzzy TV screen, and to a rising sun and some scampering kids. Perhaps Hollywood *is* the land of dreams. Either way, next time I sneak one of the kids' movies, I'll choose something less silly and more realistic—say, *Treasure Island* or *Swiss Family Robinson*.

CHAPTER ELEVEN
The Danger Garden

After wrenching my back while kicking rather viciously at some criminally tenacious weeds, I decided that it was time to learn about a new gardening subject-area: gardening *safety*. Fortunately, a website exists to educate us all about the dangers lurking among the beans, peas and weeds—SafeGardening (www.safegardening.co.uk).

Actually, I naively didn't realize just *how* dangerous modern gardening had become until I visited their website which, as they aptly phrase it, *"Was formed to offer a unique reference point on keeping safe while gardening."* Some of their sub-topic tabs showed me how little I knew of gardening perils: *Garden Trampoline Safety* ("Outta my gardens, kids!"); *Using Axes and Hatchets* (on weeds, I suppose); *Wildlife Threats to the Garden* (kids, again); and, *Chainsaw Safety* (weeds again—I like their approach to weeding).

Tales Taller than Sunflowers

Fully informed about today's green-thumber hazards, I was nonetheless unprepared for the dangers of inviting my old drinking buddy Nate over for a nighttime sampling in my garden, naturally of some homemade wine. Perhaps I should first have consulted SafeGardening's advice regarding *Garden Lighting*. More likely, though, I should have had either Nate, or the wine, out to the garden, but certainly not both at the same time!

Nate and I have had loads of fun in the past (and not a little trouble) drinking in cool places—various rooftops, an abandoned hearse, the back of a moving van headed for Texas. We had usually imbibed brewskis, but having no brewski moola *and* having this just-fermented wine, I thought it the most appropriate beverage for our little garden party since I grow no hops or malted barley, but do have fine lush grape vines garden-side. Some fruit farmer (bless his or her soul and every other thing about him or her) planted them before my time. I merely prune, pluck and ferment them.

We savored the tasty, invigorating homegrown, homemade potion as we examined (well, one of us *admired*) the garden and reminisced about crazy old times. Little did I know a crazy *new* time lay ahead of us. Yes, things soon got out of hand—or in Nate's case, out of mind.

I hesitate to say this—Nate is a big burly guy—macho not sissified. If he grew a garden it would consist of 100% habanera peppers or some similarly behind-stompin' veggies inspired by the splendid night sky.

Nate started *dancing* down the garden path.

I have flat stepping-stones rather artistically placed down that path, and he tripped on one and landed forehead first on another.

I leaned over and gently shook his shoulder saying, "Nate! Speak to me!"

To my relief, he rolled onto his back and opened his pinkish eyes.

Then he opened his mouth, and out of it came, "Those stuzid stezzing stones! Now I've got a great zain in my zoor head. What if I'm zaralyped below the waist?"

Yes, Nate had now, suddenly mixed up not his p's and q's but his p's and *z*'s.

"Here," I offered, "take my hand and I'll help you stand."

"Thanks, zal. I azzreciate that," he said.

Once we had him back on his thankfully not paralyzed legs, I questioned him further.

"How do you feel, buddy—dizzy at all?"

"Yez—dippy indeed. I feel like I'm going crapy or something!"

"Here, let's stroll around a bit," I suggested. "Put your hand on my shoulder."

You see, whenever I feel-dizzy or crazy, a wander through the veggies works wonders for me. Perhaps it would bring Nate back to his senses, as well.

As we strolled, Nate calmed down somewhat. Hoping his vocab would also rehab, I tenderly nudged him toward conversation.

"*Ah*! What a night, eh Nate?" I asked.

"Yez! It's so zeaceful—a nearly zerfect night," he said. "Zlus, this garden! I can hardly believe you zlanned, zlowed and zlanted the whole thing by yourself. I'm so zroud of you!" he added.

"Well, I didn't exactly zlow, I mean *plow*—it," I confessed, nonetheless pleased.

"No matter. It *is* zretty. And all the zroduce—you must have zounds uzon zounds of zotatoes, jalazeno zezzers, zickles and pucchinis."

As if the mispronunciation of that last veggie reminded his entrails of something, he then puked next to the pucchinis.

Waiting discreetly nearby, wondering if I should later shovel in Nate's "gift" as fertilizer, when he straightened I asked, "Feeling better now?"

Tales Taller than Sunflowers

He held up a hand, said, "Hold on a second, zartner," and wobbled off toward some nearby bushes.

"Hey! Nate! Where are you going now?"

"I'm just going over by these bushes for a minute. Zlease zardon me, but now I need to zee, too."

Fearing that one of my gardening neighbors might also be out this splendid late summer evening, I admonished, "Hey, hey, *hey*! Put your pizzle back in your pants and zip up!"

"Okay, I'll zut my zipple back in my zants, but I can't piz uz."

"Why? What's wrong now?" I inquired, newly re-alarmed.

"My pizzer is busted—it won't zull uz."

"*Oh*—well, okay buddy."

"Hey, since I just emztied my stomach, how about if you order a zezzeroni zippa from Zaza John's?"

"Nate, *one* of the reasons we're drinking homemade wine is because I'm broke. How much moola do *you* have?"

"Pero, pilch, nothing, nada not a zenny in my zocket. But speaking of wine, zerhazs we could samzle some more?"

I had to agree, and poured us a couple tall ones. After all, I rationalized, a simple, standard *slurring* would be preferable to this p-z confusion.

Tales Taller than Sunflowers

As we sat on a garden bench and imbibed, I made plans to email the SafeGardening website the next day and suggest a new category, *"Drinking in the Garden."*

However, Nate also had plans for us.

"Why don't we zack some sandwiches and zicnic in the zark tomorrow," he babbled. "Afterwards, a triz to the city poo—we can check out the tigers and liars, the zolar and zanda bears, the zenguins and pebras andmdo some zeozle watching."

"I'll drink to that," I said

Soon, Nate recovered enough to merely slur his words (he even called my wine "Purddy dammm gooood"). Shortly after that, he slumbered in the cucumber patch, *not* to be confused with the zickle zatch!

CHAPTER TWELVE
Plantism Charges Refuted!

I have always felt civilized and gentlemanly while in my garden. Politics, the daily news, banal and brutal realities, even the neighbor's irritating mutts dare not invade this haven from strife. The only controversies, *how much water and beans or carrots here*, do not cause strife or stress, do not rouse my temper *or* my blood pressure. As my veggie plants emerge from the soil and mature into healthy and lovely food-rendering entities, I experience pleasurable emotions such as joy, pride and satisfaction. Yes, my garden is a wholly pleasant place. I visit it often to escape the madness, to mulch and stake, to water and to weed.

A while back, though, while harmlessly humming and loitering, I found myself confronted by a self-righteous group of rude yet well-organized weeds. They called themselves **WOE**—

short for Weeds Organized for Equality, a branch off from the powerful Anti-Eradication League, I believe. Didactically chanting, "All plants are created equal," they accused me of the hideous character flaw of *plantism*!

I thought about defending myself by retorting, "Some plants are more equal than others," but instead I judiciously held my tongue. Why should I reply to these unkempt, uninvited upstarts? Is there no peace anywhere? So, I yanked up the activist weeds and silenced them.

Two mornings later I was accosted by a new group, **WAR** (Weeds Against Reductions, Riddance, Rototillers and Ruthless Realities). These prolific, wordy radicals did not merely accuse me of plantism. They scornfully called me a close-minded conservative, a selfish protector of corrupt self-interest. When I explained I had nothing personal against weeds, but that I favored fruit-bearing plants in my garden, they countered with shrill charges that I was furthermore an exploitative, spiritually bankrupt materialist! They said that instead of standing *on* the soil like a king, I ought to be crawling *in* it like the blind, slimy worm that I was. They strongly recommended sensitivity training.

This was way too much. I ruthlessly cracked down by yanking up these weeds as well, by their necks. I did toss and turn in bed for a few nights afterwards, but I attributed this, as well as my incessant teeth-grinding, not to the unfair accusations, but to the typically depressing news headlines.

Then tranquility reigned for a while, probably because I avoided both the news *and* my politically turbulent garden. Finally, I had to return to it (the garden, not the news). Unfortunately, the situation had escalated. I was waylaid this time by two weed organizations, the suspected terrorist group *WHY* (Weeds Who Hate You) and the more compromising, sincerely pacifistic *WAPA* (Weeds Are People Also).

The flowery *WAPA*s supported their right-to-thrive claims by pointing out that honeybees, "Those hard-working middle-Americans with strong hive values," visit blossoming weeds as often as blossoming vegetable plants.

When *WHY*'s leader, a rapid-growth thorn, labeled me "A vile exploiter of oppressed beans everywhere," I sharply replied only *my* beans were involved. Before I could add this was furthermore a mutually beneficial arrangement, the weed told me in a humiliatingly condescending tone that it had said *"Beings,* not *beans,* you unhearing monster!"

In self-defense, I yanked up the troublemakers, suffering a minor flesh-wound at the thorn of an indignant thistle, and realizing their numbers had grown to unmanageable proportions. I retreated.

As I trudged toward the house, they victoriously cried out that my occupied garden would host *AMP,* the Annual Anti-Mulch Protest next week.

They never had the opportunity. Even though I might have granted those weeds at least *some* ineradicable rights, I *did* have a garden to govern. Their fatal error was influencing, undoubtedly through insidious methods, my beloved veggie-subjects. My tomatoes began to complain about being caged, the peas and beans about being strung-up, the carrots and potatoes about being kept in the dark. In the background, I heard the influential beans whisper, "Exploiter! Totalitarian gardener!"

I finally snapped. Call me intolerant, call me a plantist if you must, but also call me a pragmatist. I pulled, yanked, hoed and tilled. I eliminated every single rabble-rousing weed and warily policed the garden every day afterward and determined if ever such dissension again reared its leafy head, I would immediately nip it in the bud and the roots if possible.

My new motto is, "The only good weed is a pulled weed."

As I mentioned, I have always experienced certain pleasurable emotions in my garden, namely joy, pride and satisfaction. But it does *not* seem fair that I should now add guilt. If ever any of the self-righteous finger-pointers leave their positions in front of cameras and make their shrill way toward my garden, I'll just meet them with *GONE*—Gardeners Opposed to Nonsensical Extremists.

CHAPTER THIRTEEN

June ... Vine ... All Delinquents!

I try to provide a good home for my vegetable plants, an orderly well-kept place where they can wholesomely grow-up straight, proud and considerate. Their home is neatly edged with clean right-angles at the corners. Their rows are straight and respectable. I've even placed flat smooth stepping stones down the middle so that no human kids sway off the path and corrupt my clean-cut veggie-kids. I stake and tie them upright, dish up the recommended dosage of nutrients, eradicate hazardous weeds, fence out molesting bunnies and pamper the darlings with loving portions of mulch. I am at my civilized best when among them. I disregard the nature-or-nurture controversy, and I allot my veggie-kids ample measures of both. In short, I raise them right.

Tales Taller than Sunflowers

Of course, not all of them toe my firm yet reasonable lines. Some act naturally wild, free-spirited, even rebellious. No, I did not sow wild oats; however, I am raising *some* spunky vine plants, squash, pumpkins and cucumbers. These demand a little more attention, understanding and bushels more guidance. Selflessly, I give it to them.

Recognizing independent types need extra room in which to roam, I allotted them a long hill of their own on garden's edge with plenty of unplanted soil between them and the more docile veggie-kids. I tried to make them feel at home, wanted, loved and understood by installing a sign that labeled this area *Vine Valley*. I babied them with deeply imbedded watering tubes. Figuring they could crawl over it to the beat of their own drummer, I even constructed an arched fence-bridge over the potatoes and nudged them toward it.

Do you suppose they appreciates this loving sacrifice, this extra-special treatment? No! They ignored it, scorned it, and defiantly grew their own ways. As it turned out, that way was every which way.

Mind you, I am not implying vine plants are the *only* troublesome plants and the other veggie-kids are leafy angels. Far from it! The peppers display spicy behavior, the broccolis sometimes appear a tad bit seedy, the beans act overly prissy and the eggplants are way too touchy. Not only that, but the zucchini can get way too big for their branches, and maturing tomatoes apparently prefer to just pull up stakes and leave! Still, I raised them with care and affection, and I experience great delight with a tinge of melancholy watching *them* mature into productive, law-abiding garden citizens.

I have no such hope for those unruly vines. Productive yes, law-abiding no! Consider the way that they sport curly mustaches. At their age! Pirate whiskers, I must presume, from the way they devoured their allotted space, cruised under and around their bridge, and pirated the space of innocent, defenseless potatoes and beans, rudely shoving them aside—the bullies!

At night when all good little plants are stretching and yawning and dreaming of honeybees, these uncontrollable vinesters prowl about poking their mischievous necks into every nook and cranny under the moon. As my mother once said, "There's not much to do besides troublesome deeds late at night, and usually only troublemakers are out and about then." How true! One night a couple weeks ago, while endeavoring a peaceful stroll down those center-garden stepping-stones, I was startled by a great commotion; There was a blood-chilling creak and spine-tingling groan, then a loud crash and a mysteriously joyful, *"Whee!"*(or two) near the potato patch. Nimbly leaping over my darling chives, I rushed over to discover several desperado butternut squash plants had indeed used my bridge, but only to party on it, apparently jump up and down on it, and merrily bring it crashing down on the potato plants!

Although I lectured them long (and sternly) for such unacceptably childish behavior, I doubt they heard me. I am a boor and a party pooper to them. Their utter disrespect was obvious later that week when I discovered some of them had run away from garden, into the neighbor's poor flower bed.

What's a gardener to do? As I mentioned, mere scolding was ineffective. I've considered standing them in a corner, or even grounding them, but I knew they'd stand for neither for long. Perhaps a good spanking would work wonders? No—that would likely only cause them to harden their precious little shells, meaning the punitive act would hurt me a lot more than it would them. My only option was to admit defeat and pack them off to a reform plot.

But I couldn't take such a measure. The reform-plot officers probably couldn't control them either, at least not without purposefully stunting them, a form of vine-abuse. And I would miss them dearly. The other, better-behaved veggie kids would miss them as well. Of that I am sure. We admit it! The garden would be an unendurably dull place without them. After welcoming back thse the prodigal squash and pumpkins and cucumber vines next year we'll all—*sigh*—just have to give them more space.

CHAPTER FOURTEEN

Matriarchy among the Marigolds

One gusty August day as I hunted insect pests in my garden, my girlfriend Maria gathered cuttings from her backyard flower patches. She wore a lovely wide-brimmed hat, but I was hatless. I must have slight sunstroke or something because as I glanced at her, I started pondering. All of the guy gardeners I know primarily grow vegetables and perhaps a few fruits. Most gal gardeners I know grow primarily flowers and perhaps a few herbs. I'm not saying this constitutes a clear gender difference. I'm not saying it because you *know* that it does.

Of course, many men have a feminine (flowery) side, and many women have a male (vegetative) side. Realizing Maria was familiar with my domain, but not I with hers, I sauntered—some might say *slithered*—over that way. Yes, I exercised my flowery side.

"Nice work, hon," I said. "Lovely flowers."

"What do you want *now*?" she asked, straightening.

"Well" I said, "It struck me that you know the names of *all* my veggie plants. I even detect a little jealousy aimed at my Black Beauty Eggplants. But I don't know the *names* of hardly any of these beauties. For example, what do you call *that?*" I asked, pointing toward a particularly pretty one off all by itself, with thick clusters of small white flowers on top of tall green stems.

"Oh, you *like* that?" She asked sounding pleased. "That's an Amazon Lily."

"How do you do?" I said, bowing toward the plant. "An Amazonian, huh? Perhaps I should respectfully call you *Madame Lillian?*"

"Let me show you more," Maria suggested.

"And their names," I said.

"You'll only forget them," she said, playfully tweaking my ear.

"Not the Forget-Me-Nots!"

"How about their *botanical* name, 'myosotis sylvatica'?"

"No wonder they changed their names," I said. "That sounded more like 'Remember-Me-Not'!"

Tales Taller than Sunflowers

"Oh, you," she sighed, starting off on our little tour, she the guide, I the tourist.

I followed behind, enjoying the view.

Proudly pointing here and pointing there, Maria expertly identified flower after flower in a singsong voice. Indeed, the litany of flower names combined into *purple* prose: Baby's Breaths and Bee Balms, Daffodils and Dendrodums, Candy Tufts and Canterbury Bells, Gladioluses and Gloriosas, Lilacs and Larkspurs and Liliums, Safflowers and Snowberries and Sun Spurges!

When she finally paused and looked expectantly for my presumably awe-struck reaction, I blurted, "What *sentimental* names flowers have! Yes, they're *lovely,* but I would've called them, say, orange blobs, purple dots, yellow frills, white wisps!"

Her brown eyes darkened browner yet.

"I thought *you* thought of yourself as a poet," she said

"Well, sure, but—"

"But, but, *but*, Mister. Your little comment reminds me of one biological fact. The largest single-cell in humans is the *female* egg. The smallest is the *male* sperm."

"Yea, sure," I agreed, "but those *aren't* brain cells or anything."

"I'll say!" she said saucily, hands-on-hips. "You've proven that *plenty* of times."

Tales Taller than Sunflowers

Boy, I loved it when her temper grew hot, but even veggies know that too much heat is a bad thing. Thinking of all the feminine names I heard during the tour—Anne, Candy, Daisy, Ginger, Iris, Susan (earthy Midwestern gals), Rosa and Marguerite (hot little Latino numbers, like my Maria), also Gladiolus, Gloriosa and Helenium (exotic, Greek, possibly *goddesses*)—I came up with a cooler line of inquiry.

"Hey Maria! All those *feminine* names among the flowers?"

"Yes?" Arms folded now, apparently cooled down.

"Did you girls name them after yourselves or vice-versa?"

"*I* didn't name anything, *pumpkin*." she said, pinching my cheek.

"Well—aren't there any *dude* flowers?" I asked.

"Yeah, but they don't smell so sweet."

"Name some!" I dared.

"Well. . .there are Bachelor Buttons, Billy Buttons, and Bishops Flowers, there's Monksheads, St. Johns Worts and. . ."

"Hey!" I interrupted, indignant as hell. "Those flowers aren't real dudes!"

"How so, *sweet pea*?" she asked, tickling me now under the chin.

"Those are *obviously* all pansies. They don't even have girl-flower friends, not any of them."

Tales Taller than Sunflowers

"How do you figure that my spicy little *chili pepper*?" she murmured, stroking my arm and then smartly smacking my rear (my, but she gets feisty within her own domain).

"Well, because one's a bachelor, one's a *Billy* not Bill or William, one's a bishop, one's a monk, and the other is a *saint*—plus, that one has *warts*!"

She moved her smooth brown face close to mine and softly said, "Well, there are Sweet *Williams*. Sweet Sultans, too. And of course *sultans* have girls, far more than you have, my cherry tomato."

"Aw, they're both too *sweet*. They're probably pansies, too, or daisies at least."

"Also, there are Golden Rods and Johnny Jump-Ups—but they're *wild* flowers."

"Damn straight they are!" I agreed, quite happy with those two comrades' wanton wildness.

"Come here," she directed, grabbing my elbow. "I'll show you some lady flowers you'll really like."

Soon, we gazed down at lovely white, funnel-shaped flowers with brilliant crimson and purple veins on top of tall stems.

"What'll you call these babies?"

"Oh—you'll like this—these are called *Naked* Lady lilies."

Tales Taller than Sunflowers

"How alluring," I agreed. "I'll bet it's these ladies that made Johnny Jump-up!"

"You bet, bulb-head," she said, winking. "Hope you enjoyed our little tour. I'm heading into the house. Maybe I'll stir something up to eat."

Off she swayed like a breeze-blown wildflower. I stood there a moment longer enjoying the view. Then I went back to the veggie garden, *my* domain, back to the perhaps commonly, but also pragmatically named plants that I admired, nothing frilly or fancy about "tomato" or "carrot" or "cabbage" or "cucumber."

I started thinking about the names of those plant kingdom (*not* queendom) giants, the trees and their names: oak, acorn, walnut, maple, spruce. *Guy*-like, even patriarchal, solid and stable as wood, not as flighty as feathers. However, I could not concentrate for long. My mind wandered. Those lush flowers certainly were gorgeous, and their scents scintillating. No wonder honeybees—all *female* bees—loiter about them so much. It was yet hot, and I soon started sweating profusely. There on my knees, I felt suddenly dirty and I was hungry for what Maria might be "stirring up."

I headed to the house and as I bolted through the door, I crooned, "Where *are* you, my Madame Maria-gold?"

CHAPTER FIFTEEN
Late Night Hot Stuff

During the day, I labor in my garden. At night, I stroll through it, unwind and relax. When the summer day's heat has gracefully subsided and the southwestern wind has calmed to a whisper or sigh, when the plants so embattled by the midday heat recover and stretch out to caress the night air for whatever moisture or magic it possesses, when the world has lowered its volume and its pace, then I visit my tranquil garden. In the privacy-fence of darkness my eyes can express what embarrasses them during the day, that I am hopelessly in love with those miraculous vegetable plants—growing, blossoming, fruiting.

My weekend-night garden visits typically include a nightcap beer with my rows of pepper plants, collectively known as *The Salsa*

Section. After the tumult of social drinking, I thoroughly enjoy a cold beer amidst my hot peppers. They sympathetically listen and do not disagree with me. A zestful yet loyal bunch, they always take my side.

The other night, the bright full moon, the ecstatic dancing fireflies, the mellow-down from a blistering 95° day to a blissful 70° night, and an overabundance of malted barley and hops from other gardens all conspired together to generate a thoroughly bewildering experience.

As I rambled toward *The Salsa Section*, I detected strident voices. I crept closer. Yes, yes there were voices, hot argumentative voices engaged in a flaming debate with exaggeration the primary rhetorical technique.

I cocked my moonlit head and overheard the youthful green chilies exclaim, "Oh yeah? Well, we're so hot that campers can rub two of us together and—*bippo!*—they soon have a blazing, crackling campfire fit for any marshmallow or hot dog or ghost story. *That's* how hot *we* are!"

"No, no—I did *not* hear that. Did not, could not have heard that," I thought.

Except I then heard the supposedly more mature red chilies retort, "Why that's nothing, nada! Did you know, for example, that when smart Eskimos go ice fishing they always take along one of us, prettier and lighter and less cumbersome than ice-augers. They simply drop one of us on the thick arctic ice and—*presto!*—we instantly melt a neat round hole right through it. *That's* how hot *we* are!"

Certainly that braggart-babble was merely my slightly soused imagination, assisted by subtle wind-puffs through overhead leaves. I yanked the tab off my last cold brew and relaxed.

Then I heard this, "You chilies green and red seem mighty chilly indeed next to us cherry peppers. We're many degrees hotter than you—hotter for that matter than every pepper else!"

Then I heard widespread laughter. I even chuckled briefly.

"Why, we're so scathingly hot that when a chef's stove malfunctions he can toss some of us under the burners and we'll readily cook-bake-broil-boil-fry-steam meals, feasts, entire banquets worthy of royalty. *That's* how hot *we* are!"

Perhaps a midnight flyer bee buzzed into my inebriated bonnet? Because now I overheard the Hungarian hots piping up in immigrant voices.

"Back in Hungary, where they really know peppers, every dwelling keeps at least one of us handy in case the furnace breaks down in winter, because we are fully capable of sending adequate heat through the otherwise chilly ducts of entire houses, buildings, and castles. That's how hot *we* are!"

Tales Taller than Sunflowers

I edged cautiously toward the more modest and soft-spoken eggplants.

Before I made it, the formerly silent cayennes, the new peppers on my hot block, yanked at my flaming ear with a drawling Cajun voice that asserted, "Yeah, yeah, yeah. Did ya'all know that when a city's power plant fails—this actually happened in New Orleans during a hurricane once—they can install dependable cayennes and we generate enough hot energy to light up the entire city, suburbs included. That's how hot *we* are!"

I chugged the last of that beer and thanked the (relatively modest) fireflies for their glimmer.

Before they could flash a *you're welcome*, I heard a spicy jalapeno voice boldly state, "Compared to us, you all are cool as cucumbers. Right this minute great scientific geniuses sip on cold drinks while pondering what to do should the sun run out of juice. Their solution? Obvious! Simply launch a bushel of us up there and—*zap!*—the solar system remains a swell warm place in which to live and sip a few cold brewskis. That's how hot *we* are!"

Now, *that* was too much, way far too much. Sure I like warm nights and cold beers, fireflies and full moons, my garden and its *Salsa Section*. Sure! Heck—having occasionally indulged in it myself, I don't dislike a moderate amount of playful exaggeration. However, I truly abhor boasting and did not know *what* to make of talking peppers. In short, I hurried out of the garden and into the house where soon I dreamed that the earth had indeed evolved into a gigantic greenhouse where cold beer was unavailable, fireflies were literally *fire*-flies and glowing hot peppers grew as big as Carolina pine trees.

Next time I partake of liquid refreshment in the garden, it will be wholesome, harmless ice water under the soothing midday sun, near the cooler heads of cabbages and lettuces.

CHAPTER SIXTEEN

Wicked Web Nets No Kids

The overheard phrase "vegetable plagiarism" grabbed my attention. Were chives imitating green onions, cherry peppers imitating cherry tomatoes? No, as I found out, that phrase was coined by comic Jerry Seinfeld as he comically discussed how his wife, Jessica, was being sued for copyright infringement because her best-selling cookbook was almost exactly the same as an earlier published cookbook. One of the many comic similarities was both cookbooks show readers how to get their veggie-hating juvenile delinquents to eat vegetables by disguising or otherwise hiding the veggies within kid-beloved fare like grilled cheese sandwiches (*not* truly beloved fare like candy and hot dogs).

Tales Taller than Sunflowers

The comic tidbit got me thinking. I did not want to add plagiarism upon plagiarism like a college freshman, but I too decided to hide veggies from kids. It wasn't *technically* "vegetable plagiarism," however, because I didn't want to hide vegetables from kids, I wanted to hide my vegetable garden from kids. I dreamed of a secret garden, a secret garden known only to me, or at least *un*known to my nieces and nephews.

Why would I want to keep my garden a secret from these youngsters? Need I tell you? Have you ever had helper kids "help" harvest green beans by yanking up entire bean plants? Have you ever had helper kids "help" weed by jerking up veggie plants that appeared weedy to their beady little eyes? Have you ever had helper kids "help" harvest by plucking every veggie in sight, ripe or unripe? Have you stood in your garden surrounded by plant-trampling juvenile heathens and reminding yourself to "Suffer the little children?"

My devout mother probably had that phrase in mind when, earlier in the season, she handed me printouts from these websites:

www.kidsgardening.org
www.gardenkids.com
www.kidsgardening.com
www.thekidsgarden.co.uk

Tales Taller than Sunflowers

Besides the fact all these sites sound eerily similar (web plagiarism perhaps) they all have the same scary thought in mind as did my mother, kids involved in gardening! I checked those sites and not one had advice on keeping kids *out* of gardens! How irresponsible of them! If this was still the cold war era, I'd have suspected a commie plot. Instead, keeping in step with the times, I suspected a *terrorist* plot.

Nevertheless, "my" garden *was* in my mother's backyard. I agreed to suffer the little nieces and nephews there. Recollect your nightmares. What resulted? Now you can imagine the number of beers it took to quell my frazzled nerves. All these sites had ideas for getting kids *interested* in gardening but, these kids were already far *too* interested. What I needed was a website to get them disinterested.

One mid-summer night, the daily gardening tasks and the nightly beers equally finished, I crept to the computer and covertly began my counter-search. I could not believe all of the websites that came up when I did a search for "gardening." It seemed more digging, planting and harvesting was taking place on the Internet than in backyards!

This gave me an idea. (I hoped and prayed that this idea would prove less troublesome than many of my previous ideas.)

Tales Taller than Sunflowers

When the kids, ranging in age from 6 to 12 and in gender from girl to boy, showed up bright and early the next day and kindly waited until I was up and about at a more reasonable hour, I gave them my pitch (call it a curveball).

"Hey, partners! If you really want to help out with this garden of ours, what I *really* need is lots of information. I don't have the time to surf the net. I don't even know *how* to surf it, to be honest. (I lied.) The first big wave of information would probably tumble me off my surfboard."

They didn't smile at this little pleasantry. They usually delighted in such acts of self-effacement, the imps.

"Now, you know where my computer room is, right?" I asked, but they all avoided my eyes, staring at the ground, refusing to admit anything. "Well, just like my—um, *our*—garden has become, that room is no longer off-limits to you. Go—*now*—and see what you can learn on the web about veggie gardening. Also find out what's new in the world of gardening, and report back to me in a month or so. Go! have fun!" I directed them.

Off they went. Twenty minutes later, they returned.

"Look what Timmy found when he searched for 'hot peppers,'" Timmy's bigger sister said, handing me a couple printouts.

Tales Taller than Sunflowers

I blushed at the nearly naked hottie barely displayed there. I stuck the printout in my back pocket for safekeeping. She sure was a *hot* pepper!

"Okay, kids, nice find—but *not* what we want. From now on, don't use search words like 'hot' or 'juicy' or 'sweet' or even 'tasty,' okay? Some adults on the web have really weird non-veggie ideas about those words."

Off they went again, glancing over their shoulders at me, giggling and whispering among their selves. When they were finally out of sight, I re-examined the evidence concerning that so-called hot pepper.

This time they stayed away for a long time, returning late in the afternoon with hands full of printouts. I immediately snatched the printouts away and examined them for further evidence. In my hands I held printouts of completed online order forms! They ordered themselves some "Lil' Tykes' Garden tools" and ordered *me* some veggie seeds with strange, vaguely disturbing names such as "Zavory Peppers," "Hansel Eggplants" and "Japanese Trifele Black Tomatoes!"

Overlooking for a moment the fact I would not for an instant plant any such nonsense in my garden, I asked, "Where did you get the money to order this stuff?"

"*Easy,*" replied Timmy's bigger sister. "We found your credit card in the desk drawer."

"Oh, *that,*" I replied, chuckling. "That won't work. It's been maxed-out. It's been over the limit, for months."

"Not anymore," she responded, smiling in a manner unbefitting her tender age. "We visited your card's website and got you a higher credit-limit. Now you're only *almost* maxed-out!"

"Well, thanks, I guess, but please don't order anything else," I said, wondering if 'almost maxed-out' meant that I had enough credit left on the rejuvenated card to get me a few beers that night. "Now go see what else you can find out for me!"

They fidgeted, shifted from foot to foot, hem-hawed and didn't go anywhere.

"Do we *got* to?" asked Timmy.

"Yeah—we're bored," added his brother Sammy (all my nephews and nieces' names end with *eee*).

"We like gardening with you more," added Sammy's little brudder.

"It's too nice outside to spend *inside* when we could be out here helping our *very favorite* uncle," said another, who to that point I thought was a neighborhood kid, not a niece.

What can you say to *that*? If the kids preferred gardening to web surfing, they were worthy of being miniaturized relatives of mine. I bent down lower and described how to tell a veggie-plant from a weed.

CHAPTER SEVENTEEN

Meeting My (Other) Self In The Garden

As I mentioned, I've been gradually earning degrees (by degrees) at a university that will remain nameless (they claim I owe them money). This past semester, hoping to better understand myself and especially, my girlfriend Maria, I enrolled in some psychology classes.

At some point in all the resultant psycho-babble, my mind snapped like a crisp Blue Lake green bean. It had to do with Freudian theory and the id-ego-superego division of the personality as a threesome. Although this seems like too *few* personalities for some of my crazier friends, for me it is way too many. Even *two* is one too many for me. I found this out when I met myself in the garden one afternoon.

Tales Taller than Sunflowers

I was slightly hung over and determined to cure my condition near the fruits and veggies of my labors. I arrived at the garden barefoot, a good book in hand and a cold beer. I sprawled down on my comfy garden-side bench and stretched my legs. I looked up and around the garden. There, at the other side of it, stood my other self, not looking very pleased with my real self. I was not in the mood for the kind of quasi-military attitude displayed by my other self, especially in my garden.

"What do you want?" I demanded. "I know what I want—tranquility."

"What a mess *you* are," the distinction made by him began. "Those shoeless feet will track dirt into the house. I just know that you again failed to put on sunscreen. And alcohol at *this* time of day?"

"Want one?" I asked, trying Gandhi's technique of peaceful resistance. And when my generosity drew an indignant glare, I muttered, "Thanks. I don't mind if I do."

Then I headed into the house, carefully wiping my feet on doormat, for another brewski. While there, I slapped on some sunscreen for tranquility's sake.

Not wanting to compromise *my*self too much with my *other* self, I remained barefooted. He still stood there, arms folded, glaring angrily from beer to bare, bare to beer. I pretended to make a cell phone call. I had to pretend because I neglected to recharge the battery, but don't tell *him*.

He interrupted my imaginary phone call (just when it was getting interesting).

"What're *we* going to do, gab and guzzle all day when there are beans and cucumbers to pick, weeds to pull and tomatoes to tie-up?"

"Oh, you'd like that, wouldn't you?" I asked.

"Like what?"

"Tying up anything or anybody."

"Oh, ha, ha! It's good to know yourself, isn't it?" He snickered through his big nose.

"Oh, I know *and* like *my* self. As for *you*, you're so full of manure I ought to chop you up and hoe you into the garden."

"Such self-loathing! What *is* your problem with, shall *we* say, your *better* half?"

"You are no fun, a spoil-sport, in fact, and that's *my* problem," I retorted.

"Well, *you* are no good sometimes. I mean, what are *we* doing still in school at *our* age, growing a garden at our *parents'* house?"

"Don't we-our-us *me*, bub!" I warned. "Anyway, education is good, right? So, more must be better, and most must be best." (I was on a roll—and, ready for another beer.) "Plus, you *know* mama *loves* fresh produce with which to work her culinary magic, something papa will not grow."

Then I left for another beer and ignored the two holes burning into my back as I walked. I returned back shoes on (the tops of my feet were getting sun-burnt). I took the offensive.

"As a matter of fact, *you* sound just like papa!" I said.

"And *you* sound just like *you* always have, like a juvenile. While *we're* growing stuff, how about *you* growing up?"

I was beginning to feel peeved, exactly what *he* wanted, no doubt.

"Why don't you educate yourself and learn that a life without fun is not worth living before you doom us both?" I asked rhetorically.

"Well, this garden, our garden," he said, "providing nutrition and saving us money, is due to *my* diligence and self-discipline, *not* yours."

"Like hell it is," I retorted. "It's due to *me* finding it *fun* and the food enjoyable. And it's lovely, and usually peaceful. Why don't you just leave you ridiculous super egomaniac?"

"Okay. If you want to live without a conscience, that's *your* problem, not mine. Before I go, I want to remind you there are many disturbing realities in today's world."

Tales Taller than Sunflowers

"Yep," I snapped. "That's exactly why I'm here today. I don't want to be disturbed by any reality other than the self-made reality of *this* world," I concluded, waving my arm in the direction of the lush greenery.

When I looked up he had vanished. I picked up my book (*Growth of the Soil* by Nobel Laureate Knut Hamsun). After awhile I put beer and book down and tied up some tomatoes, and I enjoyed it!

So when *you* visit *your* garden, leave that other self behind watching the news, analyzing the stock market, or balancing the budget.

CHAPTER EIGHTEEN
Leafy Outlaws

We all know plant activities can branch out into illicit or problematic areas. Now that harvest time has passed, I've had time to notice a recent media furor fueled by politicians' furor (or was it the other way around?) about a certain, barely mentionable plant named *Salvia Divinorum* that grew way beyond the pale into downright *criminal* pursuits. Concerned gardener-guardians of impressionable veggie-kids' morals will certainly want to keep these foul influences away from their green little darlings.

What, you might ask, have these dastardly (or worse) plants done to deserve such a reputation, not to mention proposed legislation that would make mere *possession* of them a felony? You might wonder, "Are they mutant *weeds*? Poisonous?" Here is a clue. These botanical outlaws are grown primarily in Mexico, the same Mexico where certain shade-loving gardeners cheerfully grow other villainous plants such as marijuana, coca, peyote cacti and opium poppies (no wonder the country is so colorfully festive). That's right—like those other bad seeds, *Salvia Divinorum* will no longer even be considered a plant, but instead a *drug.*

It seems that smoking or chewing the leaves of this flowering herb, now drug, until now of the sage genus and spearmint's family, can produce brief and generally pleasing visions sometimes accompanied by uncontrollable laughter. No wonder young Americans, Mexicans, Canadians, Europeans, Africans, and Asians love the stuff! But how will we ever get them back in the garden unless perchance we let them plant these *drugs* near our innocent, wholesome veggie-kids?

One study of *Salvia* users conducted by a university (and I *don't* mean a frat house) found the following to be the most common effects:

- Increased insight
- Improved mood
- Close connection with nature
- Increased sweating

Tales Taller than Sunflowers

Are *you* thinking what *I'm* thinking? Namely, that we get those same pleasurable effects from gardening, and without growing (or smoking, or chewing) *Salvia*? Or. . .were you thinking, "What if they criminalize *gardening*?" So was I.

We get no bad after-effects from gardening, other than maybe a strained lower back or something similarly minor. On the other hand, *Salvia* users also report no ill after-effects. Instead, they report a pleasurable "afterglow," or pleasant state of mind following the main effects. This is, of course, quite different from the after-effects of some (I'm not naming names, especially mine) gardeners' ~~beverage~~ drug of choice, alcohol.

I mean, scanning some *Salvia* users' reports of their experiences, among alluring titles like *A New Awareness through Salvia* and *Spinning to the Core of the Abyss,* I found this title: *My Body was an Enormous Carnival.* At the time I read this my body was a rusty junkyard (although only the night before my body was a tuneful, twinkling merry-go-round).

And, yes, vodka is made from potatoes and Bloody Marys from tomatoes' juices, yet alcohol is a *legal* intoxicant. Potatoes and tomatoes are perfectly law-abiding. Some veggies do violate the spirit if not the letter of the law, broccoli can get a tad seedy as I have heretofore mentioned, jalapenos are oral arsonists, vine plants grow way out of line, and onions and carrots and beets have formed an underground movement. Nonetheless, these activities aren't felonious or anything *like* that. Disreputable maybe, but that's about it.

Why doesn't the media fuel politicians' furor, or vice-versa (I can never figure it out) and criminalize, prosecute and execute the true felons of the plant world, the *weeds*? They at least belong behind bars, but not in our otherwise wholesome gardens. Marijuana, call it a plant or call it a drug, is actually a *weed* (or so says one particularly slant-eyed friend) but it has never bothered my garden, like crabgrass, bindweed, thistles and other invasive weeds for which I have no printable names. *These* are the true botanical outlaws. But do we get *any* police protection against them? *No!* I say that gardeners are *neglected* by lawmakers and law enforcers. And we *like* it that way!

CHAPTER NINETEEN

A Gentleman and a Squirrel

Although my carrot-top nephew insists that a "gardener snake" loiters in my backyard garden, I've long suspected a more common creature has been at work there. You see, each spring I find several young trees, typically buckeyes and walnuts, springing forth from the earth. Desiring a lush vegetable patch, not a miniature forest, I must dig-out and transplant these unexpected upstarts. I identify them by the seed-shells, attached to their roots which are usually set four to five inches deep in the ground. Did a modern day Johnny Tree-seed trek through my garden on moonless nights presumptuously depositing seeds without first consulting me?

I have found other unexplainable garden growths. Although I did not plant them, several corn plants sprang forth this year.

These I kept and tended to them just like I tend my other plants, weeding, watering, mulching and fertilizing.

I unearthed the cultivator of the mysterious treelings and cornlings on a late May watering day. As I huffed and puffed and carried two full sprinkling cans, I spotted a suspicious bushy tail above and beyond my young bean plants. The subsequent earth-shaking quality of my stomping in that direction frightened off that tail and its owner, a plump gray squirrel. As I peered into the shallow hole it dug, I found an unshelled peanut.

Immediately I deduced this just-escaped squirrel was the one who was trying to transform my garden into first a shaded lot, then into a cornfield, and now into a peanut plantation. He was a pretty smart squirrel. Undoubtedly he used all the latest, most innovative and horticultural techniques and could probably chatter me a tip or two. He did all of this, even after I set out goodies for him in the backyard! I always felt a tinge of charitable sympathy, ego-fueled pity, benevolent superiority for this squirrel, and I now saw these feelings were totally misplaced.

Then, while gently patting down soil over the peanut, I started to snicker. The squirrel was obviously not as smart and as advanced as I initially thought. The peanut would sprout *nothing*, because it had been sterilized via roasting and salting. The gray-thumber was no green-thumber.

Tales Taller than Sunflowers

How did I know the squirrel's peanut seed had been roasted and salted? That peanut had once been mine. (Not that I had planned to plant it.) Just a week earlier, the squirrel gnawed a hole through my bicycle saddlebags (some call them "panniers, but I don't know French) to pilfer the nuts stashed there. I thought it was cute at the time, but now I am a tad indignant. This squirrel was not *only* a beggar and a thief, but he was *also* a trespasser and garden-space pirate! The misdemeanors mounted.

I trembled with rage I stood near the hopelessly seedy broccoli bums, er, plants. Furthermore, that squirrel, that damn *rodent*, was a loafer, a chiseler, a cheater, an incurable tramp and unreformable repeat offender! He was a virtual burden on society or at least on me. It begged and filched my nuts and tree seeds and farmers' corn, arrogantly appropriated valuable space in my already overcrowded garden, and *then*—incredibly expected overworked me to water, weed, mulch, fertilize and harvest for him!

I resolved to henceforth yank out all uninvited seedlings and to toss them into the compost heap.

Pause . . . mental stammer . . . reconsideration.

Oh well, being a gentleman, I decided I would not act coldly and brutally, and I promised myself I would henceforth treat the squirrel's seedlings as my own. Being a squirrel, he accepted this arrangement and trustingly (not to mention *lazily*) left them to my expert care.

So, the buckeye and walnut treelings continued to get transplanted to strategic spots in the spacious yard, and they'll someday provide shade, shelter and play-space for squirrelly generations to come. Much to the envy and bewilderment of my tomatoes and Mexican sunflowers, the corn soon became the tallest garden citizens. Of course, the peanut seeds (snicker, snicker) never sprouted, nor did the cheerios the squirrel planted, naively expecting donut plants to result, I suppose.

I ceaselessly toiled over the squirrel's crops without resentment or indignation. A veggie-kid's irregular parentage ought not be held against him. The squirrel does stroll about my yard attired in distinguished gray. Rather than a no-account beast he is a gentleman at heart. Although he absolutely refuses to participate in mundane gardening chores, he does aid me by harassing the seedling chomping neighborhood bunny. Just last month, he circled and chattered at that bunny so persistently that it ran off, likely to the bunny farm, and has not yet returned. I am not yet so cynical as to assert the squirrel was selfishly protecting only his own plants. I prefer to think he protected *our* plants. Perhaps I am a fool.

When harvest-time arrived on a gusting northern wind, I generously picked squirrel's produce for him. That was our agreement, was it not? Being a gentleman, I chose to abide by it. Being also only human, I appropriated one ear of corn for my own nourishment and enjoyment. However, being a squirrel, a dastardly, black-hearted, chiseling, conniving, no-account stingy *bum* of a tree-rat, he had (I sadly discovered) planted field corn, *not* sweet corn.

I was then altogether tired of being taken advantage of by that squirrel. I decided that next spring I would plant and *abandon* corn and nuts and other miscellaneous trees, and squirrel could plant and nurture tomatoes, potatoes and peppers. For just one season, why couldnt I act squirrelly and that varmint in the distinguished gray act gentlemanly?

CHAPTER TWENTY

Terrorist Garden Plot Uncovered!

Looking for new strategies against garden insect pests one day on the Internet, I typed "garden" and "terrorists" and hit *search*. I soon found myself on a strange website operated by one who called himself a *garden terrorist*. The site was filled with vehement threats of a jihad against America's "infidel" gardens. Doubly threatened, I felt it my duty as both a gardener and as an American citizen to investigate.

My courageous email asking, "Who the hell do you think you are?" brought a cowardly email response.

"Who the hell do you think *you* are?"

Undaunted by such unspeakable rudeness and hoping to snare this snake in person, I informed him I was a reporter for

Tales Taller than Sunflowers

*Newsweek (*omitting that the *Newsweek* geeks were unaware of this) and demanded an interview. He cowardly insisted on remaining anonymous; I courageously concurred. Anyway, _____ agreed to meet me in person, at my garden. I had ~~Abdul~~ (oops) _____ right where I wanted him.

He arrived on a crisp fall day, and for privacy we sat on my garden bench. He chain-smoked clove cigarettes and kept nervously glancing over his shoulder. (Perhaps he thought there were FBI agents in the bushes.) Out of respect for his home culture, I smoked Camels that day. Then I also nervously glanced over my shoulder, because Maria had *insisted* I go job hunting, not knowing I had more pressing concerns involving Homeland Security.

Although the mostly dead November garden lay in tatters, _____ gazed at it and said, "Ah, a *lovely* sight!"

"You creeps can't claim credit for *that*," I retorted, losing all objectivity. Then, regaining it, I said, "The *Newsweek* editors will want to know of your credentials, your connections to the international terrorist network."

"Well, I once I clipped Bin Laden's toenails," he said.

"Yuck!" I responded. "Anything more *substantial*?"

"I was once interrogated by the 711 committee."

"The 711 committee? Are you sure you don't mean the *9-11* Commission?"

Tales Taller than Sunflowers

"No, 7-11. I was interested in obtaining a franchise to help fund my nefarious activities."

"Oh, okay then. Now, we *scholarly* journalists are more interested in the *why* than the *what*. So *why* wage a war of terror on American gardens?" I asked.

"We've discovered in media reports that more and more Americans are starting to garden to combat rising food costs, which is of course connected to rising fuel costs. If you infidels get your food from the backyard instead of the store, that means fewer fuel-using trips to the store and less need for all those 3-miles-per-gallon semi-trucks hauling commercially grown produce cross-country. The capitalistic scheme called supply-and-demand tells us this would cause lower fuel prices, so there would be fewer profits for us with which to wage our holey war!"

"Hold it right there!" I exclaimed. "That theory is *ridiculous*! I have a cousin who started a garden this past season just to save money. However, he bought seeds and plants, soil additives and fertilizers, insecticides, tomato cages, implements, a rototiller, freezer bags and canning supplies. He used *lots* of gas running around getting all that stuff."

"Yes, you Americans are a materialistic bunch," _____ murmured, smoking a clove cigarette with one hand and fingering a diamond earring with the other. "So how did your cousin make out?"

"He nearly went bankrupt! Just to make ends meet, he wound up selling most of his veggies and canned goods from a roadside veggie stand!"

"Ah—Allah's justice!"

"Allah? Surely you Moslems grow gardens, too!"

"Yes, but it's basically an infidel idea. Your Jesus gave gardening advice—where to cast your seeds and all that—but Mohammed *never* did!"

"Yes!" I proudly agreed. "And I will bet your guy *never* turned water into wine!"

"But, look where Jesus was betrayed—at the *Garden* at Gethsemane. By *our* agent, Judas!"

"Hang on one minute, fellah. That was centuries before Mohammed was even born."

"Yes, but Judas was an advance prophet, like, say, Elijah or John the Baptist."

I started feeling increasingly skeptical about this jerk's fantastic claims.

Getting back to the topic at hand, I said, "So, of what does your 'garden terrorism' consist? I haven't heard of any gardens getting blown up lately." I chuckled.

"Oh, we're quite a bit sneakier than *that*. This time of year, while you infidel gardeners browse through seed catalogs, we holey warriors browse through *pest* catalogs."

"*Pest* catalogs? Why the hell would you do that?"

"To select new, ineradicable breeds of vine borers, tomato worms, and also Iranian beetles—far more destructive than those wimpy Jap beetles. Then we spread them around in the garden-heavy sections of the USA!"

"Jeez now that *is* pretty sneaky," I reluctantly admitted. "What other tricks have you up your robe-sleeves?"

"Well, our chemists back in the Holey Land are developing new strains of tomato rot. And you know those little moths that fly around your broccoli plants, that leave little green caterpillars in the broccoli heads?"

"Yes."

"We call them 'Mohammed's Little Angels'."

Wanting to ask him one last tough question, I inquired, "What about last year's drought and the previous year's flooding? Surely, you can't claim credit for *those*?"

"Oh, no. Those were heaven-sent. *Our* heaven, mind you."

Then we sat and smoked awhile.

"What a *fine* animal," he said as he reached into my pack of Camels and bummed one off of me. I sat there contemplating this freakish character and his ridiculous, not to mention unbelievable, scheme.

Finally, I said, "You're not *really* a garden terrorist, are you?"

After a long silent moment, he said, weeping, "No. I'm not. What I am is a *brown thumb*. I despise you green thumbers." After wretchedly weeping some more, he peered up and said, "And you're not *really* a *Newsweek* reporter, are you?"

After a long silent moment, I said, smiling, "Yes I am."

You see, I had to keep my cover in case there ever really is such a holey plot!

CHAPTER TWENTY-ONE

Earthworms: A Foul New Scoop And Some Good Old Poop

We know science can be a business and business a science, but lately the two pursuits have taken entirely different approaches to gardeners' presumed friends, earthworms. When I mention non-veggie, nonhuman gardening friends like honeybees, I seldom—okay, *never*—mention worms. Appreciation-wise, I do not mean to keep them in the dark (although that would likely make them happy) but I almost never see the non-cute little wrigglers. Presumably, we ought to at least give them credit for aerating our garden soil, right?

However, certain scientists whom I hereby label as *worm-critics* have arrived on the scene with a foul new scoop on these heretofore harmlessly slimy little diggers who are loved by robins, fish and kids with fishing poles.

It seems, or so say the worm-critics, that worms are harming some forest ecosystems, kind of like plaque harming your teeth, I suppose. Furthermore, they reportedly can even be harmful to some gardens. That seized my attention, and I nearly decided to start a bait shop. However, looking closer at the worm-critics' alleged findings, I discovered only certain types of gardens, such as shade gardens or native wildflower gardens, might be harmed by these undercover worms. As a veggie farmer who views both shade and "native wildflowers" (i.e., good looking weeds) as *enemies*, I decided to retain my semi-affectionate (no hugging, though) feelings for my underground aerators.

I began to feel annoyed with these worm-critics. Is not anything above (or in this case, *beneath*) modern critics? Their evidence supposedly rests on two claimed facts: #1, worms alter something called (by whom, I don't know) the "duff" layer of forests by eating all the leaves and crap so darn fast.

"So what?" you ask. *"Haven't they been doing that forever?"* you further ask.

I asked the same questions until I found out fact #2: *No*, not in North America. It appears worms are *not* native to this continent, but were brought over here probably accidentally, by early settlers from Europe. So now, not *only* Native Americans but *also* Native Ecosystems (or, their guardians, the worm-critics) can apparently claim reparations from those Europeans' otherwise innocent descendants.

So, why the name *earth*worm? Does that not make them global citizens, fellow earthlings? Why not call them *Euroworms*? Or maybe we can claim this psuedo-frightening, pending eco-disaster on Martians by renaming them Marsworms? (Sounds like a potential sci-fi/horror flick; you can have the idea, gratis.)

Most of my veggie plants are *not* "native" to this land, either, nor are the Japanese beetles that wreck *many* gardeners' mini-ecosystems. Where are the critics of those? These eco-scientists want to add global *worming* anxieties to the global warming panic they've already started? As a northern gardener, I say that both worm and warm are *fine* things. In short, I say to hell with these scowling, utterly pessimistic worm-critics. It is time to turn instead to someone who sees the *bright* side of worms.

One can be either a *critic* or a *creator,* as in creator of your own garden haven. Now that I have I told you about the hysterical worm-critics, let me also tell you about someone who has created a growing business empire out of worms or, more specifically, out of worm *poop.*

Tales Taller than Sunflowers

When he was a freshman at Princeton, Tom Szaky found out from a marijuana-growing buddy just how beneficial worm poop is to most things that grow from roots. He promptly left Princeton's bull-poop for a worm-poop-as-natural-fertilizer business. His company, called TerraCycle, has since grown and grown like a weed. It does billions of dollars of business each year *without* the government backing that the aforementioned worm-critics undoubtedly receive. Perhaps you have already bought and used their pungent products?

TerraCycle's marketing takes on an especially "green" (as in eco-friendly *and* as in profitable) tinge by bottling the harvested worm poop in recycled pop bottles. I have no criticisms of this, but I do have a concern: after using the bottled worm poop, are eco-friendly gardeners then sending the now-empty soda bottles to the nearest recycling center? As much as I am a non-critic of worms, I do *not* wish to drink pop out of a bottle that once contained their poop! (Oh well. I guess I'll just keep beer as my soft drink of choice.) Anyway, if you're a gardener on a tight budget like me, you too will brighten up remembering we get our worm poop, already installed in the soil for *free*. And it's as natural as can be.

It is also *fresher*, and there is *nothing* to criticize there.

CHAPTER TWENTY-TWO

Bikinis, Bares, the Garden
(Published in *Wyoming Rural Electric News*, April 1990)

My backyard garden at one time contained some decidedly inorganic items: Lincoln Logs and whiffle-balls here, Tonka trucks and dominoes there. Seeking clues to these mysteries, I'd occasionally catch a carrot-top kid or two skipping through the fragile rows of string beans, eggplants and chili peppers. Underneath the allegedly precious little feet of those young geezers occurred an obscure yet hideous crime: mass vegecide!

Well, the vegecidal maniacs are now a year older and I am light years older. If you can't beat them—and their parents won't let me—then have them join you. Those nieces and nephews, along with several menacing-Dennis style neighborhood terrorists, I recruited as my gardening partners.

Tales Taller than Sunflowers

The desperate ploy succeeded. The novice green-thumbers now gleefully chased off rabbits and squirrels (known to them as szgwirls). At planting time they graciously, without even being asked, relieved the garden of pesky earthworms (known to them as fish-worms). The rotund little urban farmers even filled and transported sprinkler cans (this known to them as time for a water fight).

Now, these reformed horticultural criminals do not necessarily believe all plants are created equal. It is not that they love cabbages and radishes and celery less, but that they love pumpkins and sunflowers and chili peppers more. Yes, they are discriminatory, possibly bigoted, but they'll grow—like weeds—out of it. I hope.

Other plants earn if not admiration and affection then at least curiosity in those beady little eyes. Take the case of The Killer Squash. Those butternut squash are true wanderers. Mine expanded from their hill, to and through the onion patch, and finally through the marigold border out into the lawn. And still they grow. Of course in jest, I suggested to my diminutive partners that the vines might be headed for the nearby playground. Naturally, they believed me. Thus *The Legend of the Killer Squash* was planted, and it expanded even faster than the squash vines!

Tales Taller than Sunflowers

As these gardening aides are true connoisseurs of any style abundance, they most adore my garden's many bikinis? Bikinis? In the garden? Think you this some irrefutable evidence of erotic, extra-gardenary late-night activities? Let me explain: I say *zucchini*, again and again, but they always say *bikini,* and majority always wins.

This bikini presence in the garden does perhaps solve one nagging mystery. You see, one of the pink-cheeked cultivators repeatedly insists that, along with rabbits and szgwirls and a single gardener snake, he's also spied a 'bare' or two in the garden. I can only deduce that they no doubt also cultured the yet unmistakably reptilian gardener snake while innocently pulling weeds or eradicating insects, and must have created the bares by surprising and scaring their bikinis right off of them! Does that not explain everything?

Next year the garden will host some additional exotic plants. There I shall (I hope!) grow peanuts and kohlrabi and maybe even some blueberries amidst the usual tomatoes, potatoes, bell peppers and abandoned Barbie dolls. The gardening geezers will discover new sources of wonder and maybe a new legend or two. The gardener snake will have plenty of work to do. The de-bikini'd bares shall run rampant. Think of the possibilities!

CHAPTER TWENTY-THREE
A Gardening "Sir" (Not "Dude")

Over the past couple of four-seasons (please—I object to "years" references lately) I have lamentably heard myself less and less often addressed by strangers with the cheery title "dude" and more and more often audibly assaulted with the ominous title "sir." (Whether this has any relation to my lately being sometimes labeled *eccentric,* whereas before it was typically *cool*, is a puzzle I don't with which I do not to do the jig.) The last time this happened (on a day when the wind was switching to a northern gale and the leaves were turning into deceitfully jovial hues) with nowhere else to turn, I turned to my mid-Autumn garden, presumably one step ahead of Jack Frost, the pervert. Yes, I had wearied of sneaking around the local x-Mart's women's stuff looking for anti-wrinkle creams that were not labeled as such. I mean, what would come next? Would I become a *flower* gardener? It was time to either bravely face or naively escape (I wasn't sure which) supposedly inescapable reality.

Should I wear a warm jacket? I am, like most gardeners, a *summer* guy, or gal (well, not a gal despite my recent, subtly labeled x-Mart purchase) or dare I say, summer *dude.* (Who ever heard of the Sirs-of-Summer?) I certainly do not enjoy putting on a jacket, much less a cumbersome #*\>*^# coat just to visit my backyard Eden! I prefer wearing cut-offs and a tank-top, and perhaps some sunscreen, especially under the eyes. Then I begin blissfully *frolicking* like a kid to the garden, not this time of this year; not when people keep beating me over the (non-balding, non-graying, I swear) head with "Sir" and "Mister." "Uncle" is okay, at least from my younger nieces and nephews, but that's my *only* compromise. I respectfully call spring "rebirth" and mid-summer "life itself." (Veggies do not suffer mid-life crisis'.) But, dude, sir, or madam, I call mid-autumn this: #*\>*^#.

"Where did our youth go veggie dudes and/or veggie-sirs?" I wondered, zipping up my jacket as I headed to my former haven.

There I found not the usual solace. The bean plants wearily drooped as if suffering osteoporosis. The eggplants were sag-plants. My blackberry and raspberry plants were all *elder*berry plants. The chilies were as wrinkled as my cream-treated under-eyes. The sunflowers were not so towering, heads hung as if in mourning for the aging, practically *decrepit* veggie-retirees below them. In the spring had I planted or had I *buried* my oh so mortal plants? I felt like the Old Man in the Peas!

Meanwhile, my Early Girl tomatoes, I ruefully admit, had become *Later* Girls, their blush not nearly so sparkling. I have heard new fangled tomatoes that don't rot, but I conservatively submit I do not approve of them. Thinking that at least these would prove as fresh and as crisp as any northern gale, I unearthed an onion. Alas, it was thick-skinned, likely indicative of Alzheimer's or some such natural ravage.

I could plainly see with my aging if not aged eyes that the other *cool*—not eccentric—plants, the cabbage, lettuce and broccoli, were thriving man! Dude, I mean thriving! How? By chilling out! After all, adaptation, whether in veggies or humans, has definite advantages.

Whether my glass is half-empty or half-full, perhaps it is at least a *tall* glass. Standing there deciding to cool down myself, even unbuttoning my jacket, I reminded myself that canning preservation ingredients are not veggie-versions of formaldehyde; and the soon-to-be-bare rectangular garden is no oversized burial plot. I ought, I told myself, take this kinda-new "Sir" stuff with the dignity the title implies. My gourd, when I was a dude gardener, my salad days, I made perhaps forgivable, yet nonetheless laughable, amateurish errors such as letting kids too young even to be called *dude* "help" me and over-watering the garden as I over-beered myself. If experience means one ought be called "Sir," perhaps I should embrace the title.

Besides, I maturely mused, weeds and insects grow old and die too. So, how should I shaking with the chill, not age, now address them? *As sir*? *As mister*? *As madam* (when dealing with a weed or insect of the opposite sex)? Well, perhaps the helpful insects, although I'm not sure *what* to call male ladybugs, other than *confused,* should be called sir. Otherwise, I shall continue to call elderly weeds and insect-pests what I call youthful weeds and insect-pests: #*\>*^#. After calling them just that, I blissfully frolicked back to the oh so heated house (reminding myself to apply some x-Mart cream to protect against that harsh dry heat).

CHAPTER TWENTY-FOUR

The Young And The Rotless
(Published in *The American Gardener*, Nov. 1997)

Once I've spaded compost into my garden and bade it farewell until spring, my off-season activities are simple: daydream sketches of next year's garden and whatever armchair gardening I can cull from the dense thicket of available "green literature." I also sometimes play couch potato—or more accurately Lazy Boy tomato—when a gardening program sprouts from the TV.

Recently, I read a viewing guide listing for a late night nature channel special about tomatoes that don't rot. Since I uncovered the listing in the early afternoon, I had hours in which to cultivate my anticipation. You'd think that excitement would have filled me or grabbed me or at least pinched my cheek. Instead, I was seized by a gang of Bad Vibes, who ruthlessly interrogated me with troublesome questions.

For example, what uncommon fertilization techniques would we use on these incorruptible tomatoes? Manure that doesn't stink? And will we be required to sprinkle them only with water from some mail-order fountain-of-youth monopoly selling water that doesn't dry? If so, at what price? To pay for it, will we need checking accounts that don't dwindle, or credit card companies that don't bill?

Not love of BLTs but lust for profits must be behind development of these excessively dignified tomatoes, I concluded, with the help of my Bad Vibes. We can thank the eternal youth movement and its corporate wish-fulfillers: the purveyors of face lifts (bierpharoplasty) and nose jobs (rhinoplasty), tummy tucks and fanny fakes, implants of teeth and hair and breast bulk. Now that they've reversed all outer signs of human wrinkling and sagging, bulging and balding, they've aimed their greed-glazed gaze at aging tomatoes (lycoperisplasty).

I know several confused boys and girls with parents who are constantly mistaken as their slightly older siblings. Where does it all end? I mean, the Parthenon is crumbling. Are we all to outlast it and our vegetables too? I propose that a tomato should look like a tomato and should furthermore act its age.

Tales Taller than Sunflowers

Of course, a certain party at my house who frequently objects to the inevitable springtime topsoil shoeprints on her majestic carpet might brighten at the news of these tomatoes that don't rot. Surely, she'll hope, garden soil that doesn't track can't be far behind.

Unlike my Bad Vibes and me, she'll not consider the negative effects. For instance, how will the hyperactive neighborhood imps react when deprived of their annual rotten-tomato wars? We certainly can't allow them to hurl immortal, stenchless-manured, dryless-watered tomatoes now, can we?

Even many non-gardeners (*brutes*!) grow at least a tomato plant or two each summer. By decade's end we could face a tomato population explosion crisis. My Bad Vibes and I foresee violence and anarchy. Even virtuous, red-juiced Early Girls and Better Boys may not escape unscathed.

Natural processes are supposed to be gardeners' friends. Consider what foul influences those unnaturally self-centered tomatoes could exert. We envision compost that doesn't decay, annuals that don't go to seed, honeybees that don't work—in short, gardens that don't grow!

While conversing with these philosophical, somewhat longwinded Bad Vibes, I missed the TV show. Its hour had passed, and that was just hunky dory with me. It'll never take hold anyway, at least not on my plot of earth, or at least so I decided after kicking the Bad Vibes out. After all, tomatoes that don't rot sound suspiciously like what we already have at the supermarket, tomatoes that don't taste. The trendsetters should focus their energies on more practical matters such as vines that don't climb and jalapenos that don't burn.

CHAPTER TWENTY-FIVE
Not the Garden of Eden

Here it is, the dead white depths of a frigid winter, and not only am I dreaming— *nightmaring,* actually— of gardening, but I am dreaming of gardening during one of Mama Nature's other unkindly moods, a drought. It must be all this dry furnace heat, so warmly wrinkling the tender skin beneath my roving eyes, bending my pliable mind that dry direction.

The drought I dreamed was one of biblical proportions, far bigger and more disastrous (at least to me) than was the infamous "dust bowl" of the 1930s. I first learned of that drought in Steinbeck's novel, *The Grapes of Wrath.* Speaking of grapes, which in my case means speaking of *wine,* during this particular dry season I would've (if I could've) turned my wine into water!

Tales Taller than Sunflowers

This arid summer I was invited, prodded, urged and begged to toil some of my brother's country spread where he grows a garden big enough to feed his four kids, with work big enough to keep three adult kids extremely busy under *normal* conditions. But this summer it was far more parched than normal. Day after day after (imagine three dots into infinity, here) it was endless summer.

It was even worse than the prior year's ceaseless *rain*, when I felt like *Noah*, but with an empty ark. (I would've had so little produce to feed the floating paired beasts, they would've soon pounced upon and devoured each other.) Anyway, Jesus wisely advised to plant your seeds on good ground, and at my brother's we religiously did so. However, parables are by definition simple, so Jesus could not go into questions of *water,* but if he had he would have wisely agreed that seeds need water just as much, if not more, than good soil.

We prayed for rain. No rain came. It got so bad that I could not even sleep on my waterbed, feeling guilt about the abundance beneath me and dread about the dreams of draught awaiting me.

Unfortunately, my brother placed his garden too far from the house to run even a firefighter-length hose. Fortunately—sort of—he placed his garden not far (about 25 yards) from his pond which, although lowering daily, still held all the water we needed and could carry. (Did I *really* say "not far"?)

Tales Taller than Sunflowers

We, meaning I, dipped a five-gallon bucket into the pond, strained to lift the (half-filled) bucket, and staggered to the garden, which seemed to recede more quickly than my hairline as I approached it. The kids say I called for God numerous times on these strenuous trips, but I (probably in some sort of flagellant type religious frenzy) do not recall this.

As I set down the bucket, I'd shake myself like a wet mutt so as to spray my copious sweat on any nearby shriveled plants. Then I'd dump the water into a twenty gallon cooler sitting there (lucky thing) for just that purpose. From there, the "waterers," my sister-in-law Tammy and her three young daughters (my brother worked evenings or I would've been a waterer) gathered like biblical maidens about an ancient well and scooped water out with half-gallon containers, splashing some out every time. They sped off to water the waiting plants, spilling more precious water as they went, and hurriedly dumped it over wilting plants so rapidly that most of it ran off to distant parts before the arid soil could absorb it.

The fourth child, an ornery and obese toddler, hung around, like his uncle often does, next to the cooler. He played with his rubber froggy floating in the muddy water and splashed out as much of that as he could, thus contributing in his chubby little way to the overall water wasting efforts.

Tales Taller than Sunflowers

Off I'd march with empty bucket to the pond—which I wanted to dive into and forget this whole ordeal—then, more slowly, back again with half-full bucket. Being only one water carrier supplying four water spillers and one tiny water splasher, I had to keep determinedly at it lest the cooler ran empty. (Drought or draught, it has *always* been my policy to *never* let a cooler run empty!)

On one return trip I found the toddler had climbed in the cooler and turned it into his own private Jacuzzi. On the next return trip, I discovered he had abandoned his Jacuzzi by upsetting it so that he could sample some nearby green onions. I went into another—shall we say—religious frenzy, or at least so say the older kids, who were warned by their mother to not repeat a single word of it.

On the return trip after *that*, I saw all three of the waterer kids were gathered around a *flower* patch, watering those non-veggie plants like God watered the world in Noah's time. I feared flooding in the flowers!

"*Kids!*" I ~~screamed.~~ *shouted,* I mean.

They looked suspiciously my way. I *had* been grumpy lately.

"No need to water the flowers," I began in a kinder, gentler scream. "Those are to become *dried* flowers anyway. No, what I'd like you sweethearts to do, if you *really* want to help, is to make a circle and bow your heads and *pray for rain*."

They gazed dubiously up at the broad expanse of sky, perhaps looking for inspiration, but not for clouds. Having thus imparted religious guidance to the young souls, I went wearily off for yet another bucketful to be splashed, spilled and generally wasted away. As I went, I noticed the toddler had watered two onion plants, industrious little dude that he indisputably is. Then I also noticed that he had slung his sopping diaper off nearby. Oh ~~hell...~~*well*, I mean.

I heard strange whooping sounds as I labored back with yet another half-bucketful. Arriving on the scene, I found the puny pagans had abandoned solemn prayer in favor of a rousing rain dance.

When they finally stopped, I sternly admonished, "*Pray* for rain, you *heathens*!"

"We pray afore we eat and afore we sleep," the middle-sized pagan impudently replied. "We *dance* for rain!"

"Plus—we're *thirsty*," added the oldest one, who was none too old.

"Okay, okay," I said, playing the kindly uncle.

Out of the nearby shade I pulled a plastic jug about 1/3 filled with drinking water.

"Don't drink *all* of it," I warmly warned the youthful laborers.

"Hey!" said the mouthy mid-sized one, gazing at the dirt-smudged jug. "How *old* is this here water?"

I started to reply, "About three hours," then stopped and thought. *Hmm* ... Finally, I grandly announced, "*That* water—why it's *millions* of years old!"

"*Millions?*" they repeated in unison, eyes wide and pointed my way.

"Yep," I affirmed. "*That* water was in Noah's flood, was part of the water that God parted in the Red Sea (these kids knew their Bible stories, sometimes even calling me "Judas" behind my back), was once walked on by Jesus, was even used by God to water the Garden of Eden," I elaborated. Unable to stop this fun stuff, I added, "It was even in the iceberg that sank the *Titanic!*"

They looked at the jug of water as if it was a sacred relic.

"Can we still *drink* it?" the mid-sized one asked reverently.

I was still trying to decide when their mother showed up and said, "Yep! Drink up, all million's years worth."

Then, she took me by the elbow and said, "Enough of this for now. We'll just preserve by drying rather than canning and freezing this year, if necessary. Let's gather the kids (glancing about until she located the toddler, back in his Jacuzzi) and then go water ourselves with some one-year old wine. And, no; it's not *dry wine*."

Such good sense is one big reason I love that gal.

That night, as we older kids drowsily watched a movie set in the (how appropriate) desert, the younger kids romped and frolicked, as is their due. Only the toddler slept, undoubtedly dreaming of long-gone mud puddles. Suddenly, for the first time in weeks, we heard thunder. It sounded again, and again. Soon, that unfamiliar old rooftop pitter-patter gloriously began.

Out on the porch, where we all went to watch and revel, I murmured, "Our prayers were answered."

I felt a tug on my wrist. It was the mid-sized one.

"No," she said. "It was our *dance*."

CHAPTER TWENTY-SIX
Waiting On Global Warming

Now that snow thoughtfully blankets my chilly garden, now that the past summer's produce sits safely in mason jars and freezer bags, *now* I can contemplate next year's garden, not that this year's garden required improvement. Helped by both ideal rainfall and an unusually late season-ending autumnal frost, it produced a virtual bumper crop.

Yet, what nature bestows nature can withhold. A late-spring frost and early-autumn frost next season could mean an extremely brief life span for my veggie plants. A late May frost. not unheard of, could even cut them down in their youth. What, me worry? Yes! Several gardening friends of mine have built small greenhouses for safe early planting, but they have money and space I lack. If only my entire yard was a greenhouse . . . .

Tales Taller than Sunflowers

In the winter I follow the news a bit more, perhaps to prove to myself other people have problems too. If I ever also acquire some gardening news this way that's an appreciated if rare bonus. Imagine my interest, then, when I read *this* heading: *DiCaprio Goes Green*. Always interested in celebrity gardeners (well, *any* gardeners), I read more.

Paragraph one informed me DiCaprio "lobbied loudly" for clean water for all. Well, I understand a green-thumber needing water, but he lives in southern California, which has no fresh water! Do they want ours? What would they trade us for it—earthquakes? I have, in fact, heard some Californians want a water pipeline from our Great Lakes. For what do they want it? Gardens don't need clean water. Furthermore, most actor-activists drink bottled water, not tap water. If they want our water to wash their limousines and Ferraris, they can forget it. I say we only pipe them water during flood years. I will certainly donate *my* excess H_2O. I also say if DiCaprio's crowd desires more water, they ought to desert that desert for more natural human-life locales (like the Great Lakes region).

The next paragraph confirmed DiCaprio was not so much "going green" as "turning red." Apparently, the article heading "green" meant not the kind of green found in gardens, but the kind of green folded into money-clips. Yes, he *is* making yet another movie, but about *global warming!* Sitting near my favorite heating duct, I eagerly leaned forward and read onward, suddenly tremendously interested.

According to DiCaprio, "Global warming is ... one of the most important issues facing humanity." I'll say! So will any other northern gardener surrounded by snowy horizons and fretting about short growing seasons. But promises are all we get. We hear and hear about this alleged global warming, but where the hell is it? We (and our veggies) shout, *"Give us global warming NOW!"*

I mean, we also hear lots of talk, talk only, but oodles of it about a more equitable distribution of wealth. We say those actor-activists can keep their wealth and squander it freely. What we non-actor, non-activist northern gardeners demand is a more equitable distribution of *warmth.*

Cool veggies like onions, lettuce and broccoli might sulk awhile, but think of the other veggies! Consider the greater good. How much more productive, not to mention *enjoyable,* would a nine-month growing season be? Longevity would arrive like a summery Santa for warmth loving tomatoes, peppers and eggplants. We could grow stuff that now we cannot, not without, well, without a *greenhouse,* neat stuff like yams and pineapples, like orange trees and banana trees.

Tales Taller than Sunflowers

Hollywood gardeners can (of course) already grow such stuff (that is, if they can unearth sufficient fresh water for them). Why should they care that we cannot grow such goodies? And why should we care if the long-anticipated, even *prayed for* (by religious gardeners) "greenhouse effect" finally grants us a long growing season and by melting the polar ice caps, grants them all kinds of water (admittedly *salt* water) in the form of coastal flooding? We wouldn't object to nearer ocean beaches at which to enjoy the longer summer and relaxing in the sun after extended season gardening chores.

Face it. Global warming results in large part from carbon monoxide emissions, and places like L.A. and similarly sprawling coastal cities put most of it into the air (we'll thank them later). My own cigarette pack warningly and clearly states, 'CIGARETTE SMOKE CONTAINS CARBON MONOXIDE.' So why don't these the city-limit signs of these cities say, 'THIS CITY'S AIRSPACE CONTAINS TONS OF CARBON MONOXIDE?'

As I mentioned earlier, we will thank them some day, some warm and balmy December day as we stand amidst head-high pepper plants, someday after their long-promised, not-yet-delivered global warming has at long last arrived. I believe these type of people claim that saving the whales is of supreme importance, but how many whales have they personally saved? Meanwhile, I have through great effort saved *many* veggie plants from untimely frosts. If the greenhouse effect would finally get here I'd have more time and energy to also save the undoubtedly darling whales.

You see, what we northern gardeners fear far more than global warming is global *cooling*. Have you ever tried to grow veggies in an ice age?

CHAPTER TWENTY-SEVEN
Gardening Cons

It is no longer enough to simply say you have a "vegetable garden" or—on a lesser note—a "flower garden." No, in this age of specialization you need a *special* name indicating some purpose other than merely feeding yourself or beautifying your backyard. Some of these special names have to do with specific culinary tastes. The *Salsa Garden,* for example, consists of tomato and pepper plants, as well as onion, garlic, and maybe cilantro plants. I've also heard of *Pizza Gardens,* with pretty much the same plants, but instead of cilantro, they have oregano and basil, pepperoni and cheese gotten elsewhere. The pizza garden can look really cool and it can be planted in a circle with dissecting paths marking the "pieces." Some people call a garden right outside their kitchen (ready?) a (surprise!) *Kitchen Garden*. I suppose I could call my garden a *Vegetable Soup Garden*, but I don't dare be that cool.

Many people, for unfathomable reasons have no garden, but do take great care of their lawns, grass and bushes. These have been titled, probably by those who sell them tons of lawn-care stuff, *Yardeners*. I guess that means their lawns ought to be called *Yardens*, right? You can tell a true *Yarden* by its lush, manicured grass and hedges and by its patio, barbecue grill, fine lawn furniture and perhaps birdbath. There are no real kids, who could make paths on the grass and tunnels in the hedges and scatter toys everywhere. I have *never* seen a yarden that I *didn't* want to turn into a garden.

Enough of trivialities! After all, some other gardens have names that indicate not only a special purpose, but also a *higher* purpose. For example, *Victory Gardens* are making a comeback. The original *Victory Gardens* thrived during World War II when people waged war from the home front by supplementing their food ration coupons with homegrown produce. This theoretically freed up more food for the troops, although I don't think any of these patriotic gardeners grew tinned beef or biscuits. *Victory Gardens* are making a comeback because of the war against higher prices, although I know that none of these current patriotic gardeners can grow gasoline.

Tales Taller than Sunflowers

I've also heard of *Healing Gardens,* typically grown on hospital or rehabilitation-center grounds. The idea is that a stroll or wheelchair-ride through the garden will work wonders for the patient's morale, a fine idea! I am thinking of growing a small *Healing Garden* next to my vegetable garden, so that I can stroll or limp through its healing powers after the nights that I use my vegetable garden as a *Drinking Garden.*

Now penal institutions are getting into the act. A number of them in Missouri, Florida, New York and other states are allowing or forcing inmates to grow prison-yard gardens that they call *Justice Gardens* or (more creatively) *Jail Gardens.* Certainly, the prisoners will gladly trade the task of breaking up rocks with pick-axes for the pleasure of breaking up soil with hoes.

I'd imagine that those well-behaved inmates who are in for reform purposes get to plant, tend and harvest the veggie plants; and that those bad-apples who are in solely for purposes of punishment will have to do the weeding. Some of these felon farmers even say that after they get paroled (or break out, whichever comes first) they'll continue to garden on the outside. I think that's *great!* Now, instead of stealing veggies from the gardens of us solid citizens, they'll grow their own. Instead of distributing marijuana, they can diversify by growing it.

Tales Taller than Sunflowers

They have to be careful, though, and not just about their marijuana gardens. Simple over-watering or under-weeding may become parole violations. New Zealand has *Justice Gardens* in some of their prisons. However, I recently read a New Zealander gardener, while digging in her garden, found a *bomb*. What if a New Zealander ex-con gardener found a bomb in his or her garden? Surely, possession of a bomb, however innocent, would be a parole violation! Then he or she would go back to trying to grow experimental glazed donut plants for the guards, desperately hoping to find yet another bomb in the *Justice Garden* with which to break out.

Here in America we are more forgiving. We encourage those who overcome past transgressions through the wholesome activity of gardening. If you want to locate an ex-con gardener and encourage or advise him or her, how could you identify him or her? Here's how: first, look for a gardener wearing an orange jump suit without a picket fence, but instead a barbed-wire fence surrounding the garden. And where you'd have a patch of Better Boy and Early Girl tomato plants tied to stakes, they'll have *Badder* Boy and *Early-Release* Girl tomato plants either *chained* to stakes or simply caged. Where you'd look all around, stretch, and exclaim, "*Ah*—the great outdoors!" they'll look over their shoulders, slouch, and shout, "*Ah*—the great outside!"

Tales Taller than Sunflowers

What advice could you give them? Tell them that bad bugs cannot be reformed, and that the vagaries of Mother Nature are as inescapable as those of her sister, Lady Justice.

CHAPTER TWENTY-EIGHT
A Date To Forget

My junior gardening partners sometimes suggest I grow some different plants than what I do—peanuts, for example, or Kiwi fruit, in other words, plants that I *would* grow if only I could. Recently, one of them, for gourd knows what reason, asked me why I do not grow *dates*. Only after explaining that dates grow in desert-like conditions, not near-arctic conditions such as exist in still-waiting-for-global-warming wintertime Ohio, did the memory hit me—the memory of my own pre-gardening (pre-civilized) days when I experienced a true *date from hell*, a memory formerly suppressed in a back-of-mind drawer labeled "Dates to forget."

I am thinking of a time when, as a bold and spirited young California man, in other words, *not* yet an earthy gardener but instead a flighty flake, I would eagerly seek out dates in places both typical and unusual. Some dates turned out good, some dates turned out bad, other dates simply did not even turn up, but none ever qualified as a *date from hell*, a date from purgatory perhaps, but not a date from hell.

Then my glass-sculpting cousins from LA telephoned and informed me they'd soon hawk their wares at something called "The Indio Date Festival."

A *date* festival? How refreshing! Singles bars had lately seemed too impersonal for my tastes, swingers' clubs of course way too wild, TV dating shows far too public, personal "seeking" ads too risky, and singles' cruises absolutely too expensive. The idea of a *date festival* conjured images of square dances, hayrides and senior proms. It seemed wholesome, red-blooded . . . naturally, I resolved to attend.

What a place for it, though—the middle of the scorching desert. Oh well, the dry heat would at least minimize the possibility of embarrassing, date-repelling underarm odors. Also, the desert moon might inspire romantic passions. All things considered, the desert seemed to be the *ideal* locale for a date festival.

Unaware I'd soon prove myself a fool in love anew, I got a good night's sleep, devoured a light yet ample breakfast, dressed in cheerfully colored light cotton clothing and optimistically set out. I did not take along a date and hoped to find a like-minded one there.

By early afternoon I arrived. Great crowds milled about without scent of underarm protestation. The sun smiled down on us like a sympathetic and understanding chaperone. I knowingly winked up at it.

Then I sought out my cousins' booth, appropriately labeled "Artistry in Glass." While complimenting them on their impressive array of lovely glass sculptures—sharks, roses, unicorns, roses—I inwardly resolved to later return with my new-found date and purchase one of these for her. Wouldn't her eyes sparkle at that?

My own eyes, more pragmatic, darted about at the passing if not *surging* throng. There appeared to be many attractive bachelorettes among the many pre-dated couples, also a fair number of bachelors who were my competition.

My worldly cousins reassured and encouraged me that "There were plenty of dates here for everyone."

In search not of plenty, but only one, I gallantly set out.

The Date Festival organizers spared no excess in mood-enhancing treats. Various vendors offered relevant snacks: stuffed dates, chopped dates, nutty dates, candied dates, date bread, date yogurt and date milkshakes.

Getting into the spirit of the occasion, I sampled them all. I even tried the tasty date-milkshake twice. As I sipped, I envisioned myself sharing one later with a sparkle-eyed date in the old-fashioned cheek-to-cheek two-straw style. That vision so delighted me that I soon returned for yet a *third* date shake.

As I polished that off, a lovely dark-haired beauty caught my eye, and I hers. Unfortunately—*tragically*—my tummy suddenly revolted. How could I act glib and smooth, much less romantic, while suffering nausea? I could not. The opportunity slipped away.

I feigned interest in the fairway vending tables while waiting for the tummy troubles to pass. . . after that, watch out!

Suddenly, a charmingly simple table of plain, unadorned dates attracted my attention, no frills or fakery here. They seemed refreshingly natural and adoringly simple, innocent and virtuous like (I now know) Early Girls and Better Boys.

Ignoring the premonitory tummy trouble, I grew excited. Alas, excitement for me typically led to disaster, and this would prove to be no exception.

Perhaps the desert sun had pounded down on my head for too long. Maybe the beer I foolishly drank the night before had lingering effects, clouding my judgment. Possibly, I merely lost my patience and could not remain dateless one more second.

Either way, I chose a certain date, my *date from hell* to be. This date held a certain mysterious appeal. I could put my finger on it (the appeal, not the date). I've always been drawn to surface innocence. To tell the truth, I'd never made wise choices regarding dates.

Anyway, this was a bad date, very bad, a virtual fruit fatale!

Oh, I swallowed it like a man. Couldn't stomach it, though. I didn't feel sorry for myself afterward, no remorse or self-pity. However, I did swiftly sprint behind the nearest structure where, although my heart did not break, my stomach did empty.

I spent the rest of that ill-fated afternoon moaning and groaning in my cousins' camper. Outside the murmuring throng passed by, dated couples and dateless singles, many of them enjoying what I never again would, date milkshakes.

Good luck to them. Good luck, and farewell! I departed the festival in the early eve and headed stoically back to the glittering city. Within the year I returned to the good old Midwest where a date is a date and a garden a garden, with vegetables, not dates, not unless my earthy Midwestern girl Maria strolls through it with me.

CHAPTER TWENTY-NINE
A Growing Outside-In Mess

During the waning weeks of Winter, as March wavers between lion-like and lamb-like moods, my gardening activities are few: fussing with my garden blueprint, shopping for seeds, and window-shopping for implements. As those activities lack action, I also sometimes venture outdoors to actively admire the temporary weedlessness of my (likewise veggie-less) garden patch, or to vigorously shake my fist at the gray sky and energetically curse Mother Nature as a frigid you-know-what.

Meanwhile, my decidedly non-frigid girlfriend Maria warmly—if not *hotly*—starts her flower garden indoors late each winter, as if to prod Spring nearer. She has an elaborate system rigged in an otherwise unused bedroom. Fluorescent grow lights that dangle from the ceiling on adjustable chains, an automatically timed sprinkler system, and heating pads she calls "bottom warmers" under seedling trays all contribute to her success. Although she starts mere flowers here, I am impressed.

I was over one mid-March day, bothering her or keeping her company (I am never sure which) pretending to admire her young flowers with their artsy-fartsy leaf designs, when I noticed that they were sprouted out of something other than soil.

"Hey! Marie!"

"Hey! *What?*"

"You don't have the real dirt in these containers. Your flowers will *starve* to death."

"Oh—I use a starter mix of peat moss, perlite and vermiculite, instead. It's called a 'soil-less mix,' amateur."

"I'd call that a *soul*-less mix," I retorted, a little irked that this high-tech approach reached into the very soil. "Didn't Jesus say to cast your seeds on good *soil*?"

"I didn't exactly *cast* my seeds, *reverend*. Plus, the only thing holy about you are your jeans."

Then, noting some empty (other than the soil-less stuff) plant trays off to the side, I pointed and sympathetically asked, "Aw—no luck with those, huh?"

Tales Taller than Sunflowers

"Actually," she replied, unperturbed, "I've planted all of the seeds that I'll need—those trays are extra, for now."

Hmmm, I thought. I was frankly sick of all this wintertime non-activity. Perhaps I could start some veggie seeds here?

I decided to butter her up some before popping the question. Waving at the entire set-up, I said, "I must admit, dear, this is the very finest indoor garden I've seen since Eddie Kincaid's!"

"Eddie Kincaid? Hey—isn't he in *jail*?"

"Right you are, as usual. In his indoor garden, he grew flowering weeds that were, as it turned out, highly illegal."

"Wish *all* weeds were illegal," she said, smiling.

"No kidding. Heck, I'd even join the police force. *You* like men in uniforms, don't you?"

"Um—depends on which uniform and what man, soldier."

Cuddling closer, I made my pitch.

"Hey rose-cheeks, how about if I put those empty trays to good use by starting some *veggie* plants in them?"

"Sure, sweet pea—take all you want!"

"Um—but I've no grow-lights, no sprinkling system, no bottom warmers."

"You've got a bottom warmer—*me!*" she said in that oh-so familiar, slaphappy voice.

I strategically backed a small distance away, saying, "You know what I mean. How about if I start my veggie seedlings right here?"

"Well," she stalled, shifting from foot to foot. Then, finally standing still for once, she said, "Okay, I guess. But that means you and your plants will be my *tenants*. Rent will be three back-rubs and two foot massages a week, and late penalties will be *severe*."

"Agreed!"

"And—*strictly* enforced rules: clean up after yourself, and in eight weeks, out your plants go and out *you* go too."

"Aw, Maria, Baby ..."

Out of sheer gratitude, I promptly gave her the first soothing rental payment. The next day I returned with packets of pepper, tomato, and squash seeds and a bag of *real* (potting) soil, but before I, much less my *seeds*, could get started, the rather impressive landlady protested.

First, it seemed my soil-bag had a small leak. After cleaning up *that* mess, I heard about why only soul-less "dirt" was allowed in Maria's grow-room—something about pathogens and something called "damping off," I forget the specifics, but Maria always wins with me, so I agreed to double-bag my just-evicted dirt and take it with me when I went.

Tales Taller than Sunflowers

Then she poked fun at my defenseless seeds. She called them "commercial store bought" seeds and suggested that the resulting produce would as-a-result taste more like (horrors!) store-bought produce. She also proudly informed me she exclusively used, I thought, *earlobe* seeds.

"*Earlobe* seeds? What the heck are *those*?"

"*Heir-loom*," she re-pronounced it in an alluringly sexy schoolmarmish way as she playfully tweaked my earlobe. "That means I use the seeds from my best flowers each year to start the next year's flowers. A lot of my flowers this year will be descended from flowers I grew five years ago."

"Oh, why didn't you just say so," I said, happy in my own down-to-earth simplicity, secure in the knowledge nothing from the store could ever taste like my home-grown veggies this year or any year.

Maria helped me get my seeds started, and then we teamed up on a scrumptious pasta dinner. After that we snuggled and watched some romantic comedies that made our own life seem somewhat normal. During all of this, I paid the entire week's rent. However, she raised my rent! I happily supplied two weeks in advance.

Our joint outside-in gardening venture started off well, but such domestic bliss, alas, cannot always, can perhaps *never*, last. As

Tales Taller than Sunflowers

April reached us and progressed, as our seedlings likewise progressed, our relationship slowly regressed. For one thing, Maria thought I spent way too much time in the grow-room, even though I explained to her my breathing provided her and my young plants with necessary carbon dioxide. She also objected to my very occasional cigarette smoking in there, even after I explained to her that, this way, the developing veggie plants could gradually adapt to second-hand smoke, which they'd later experience first-hand from the garden-area barbecue pit.

    Arms crossed and lips pursed, she remained unconvinced. And then as I was transplanting my growing veggie seedlings to bigger pots one day, I dribbled some soil-less soil and watery water on the florid floor in front of her increasingly dark brown eyes. I felt, in front of my goddess, like a slobbess. Oh, when would warm weather—the outdoor season—arrive?

    The last straw—and I don't mean as-in berry—came when my juvenile squash plants grew so big, like elephants in the presence of gazelles, that they crowded and shaded her dainty little flowering upstarts. She moved them away—out of the light.

    I moved them most of the way back.

    She moved them even further away.

    Finally, even though I'd paid rent for months in advance, she suggested I move my plants outdoors, and myself with them!

"Anyway, it's high time for spring *cleaning,*" she announced as she opened a window to a splendid early May day.

"I'll help!" I offered, determined to regain and retain her priceless affection.

"*You,*" she began, "had better go and tune-up your rototiller, clean up your gardening tools, and straighten up your tomato cages."

"Aw—it'll be lonely work for both of us."

"I'll be out there in awhile," she promised.

And she was—in a swell, brand new sun hat. She also had me over for dinner that night, made from last year's garden's preserves, and even she admitted it did not taste at all like store-bought stuff. I was far more comfortable as a guest than as a tenant, but I nonetheless paid her advance rent toward next year's outside-in growing season.

About The Author

Steven Butterman is the author of:

Bicycle Touring (1994: Wilderness Press, Berkeley)
Ride Guide: Ohio's Covered bridges (1999: Anacus Press--co-authored)

Periodicals--American Gardener, Catholic Forester, Inland, Paperback Parade, Mansfield (Ohio) News Journal, Baja Times co), *The Art of Music,* Desert Skies, Hartford Woman.

Education:

B.A. (English Literature) The Ohio State University (2001)
M.A. (Creative Writing) Eastern Michigan University (2004)
M.A. (European History) Eastern Michigan University, pending

Ohio State: co-founded, served as initial managing editor, and contributed to a literary annual, "Immaculate Cauldron." Winner of an unprecedented number of undergraduate writing awards for (Mansfield) campus--Essay, fiction, and poetry.

www.ingramcontent.com/pod-product-compliance
Ingram Content Group UK Ltd.
Pitfield, Milton Keynes, MK11 3LW, UK
UKHW022231230426
12048UKWH00016BA/1197